LISA B. KAMPS

BLUE RIBBON

SUMMER

LISA B. KAMPS

LISA B. KAMPS

BLUE RIBBON SUMMER
Copyright © 2015 by Elizabeth Belbot Kamps

All rights reserved. Except for use in any review, the reproduction or utilization of this work in whole or in part in any form by any electronic, mechanical or other means, now known or hereafter invented, including xerography, photocopying and recording, or in any information storage or retrieval system, is forbidden without the express written permission of the author.
The Baltimore Banners© is a fictional professional ice hockey team, created for the sole use of the author and covered under protection of copyright.
All characters in this book have no existence outside the imagination of the author and have no relation to anyone bearing the same name or names, living or dead. This book is a work of fiction and any resemblance to any individual, place, business, or event is purely coincidental.

Cover design by Jay Aheer of Simply Defined Art
http://www.jayscoversbydesign.com/

LISA B. KAMPS

All rights reserved.
ISBN: 1515075761
ISBN-13: 978-1515075769

BLUE RIBBON SUMMER

CONTENTS

COPYRIGHT 5
DEDICATION 11
OTHER TITLES BY THIS AUTHOR 13

ONE 15
TWO 22
THREE 31
FOUR 39
FIVE 48
SIX 56
SEVEN 62
EIGHT 70
NINE 74
TEN 85
ELEVEN 94
TWELVE 99
THIRTEEN 109
FOURTEEN 116
FIFTEEN 124
SIXTEEN 134
SEVENTEEN 141
EIGHTEEN 150

ABOUT THE AUTHOR 15959

LISA B. KAMPS

For the men in my life:

Jack, for years of support and laughter and trying times and living life and the whole package--having you with me has made it all worthwhile!

Gerrit, for your stubbornness and silliness and determination that keeps us on our toes, keeps us worrying and keeps us laughing.

Connor, for your insight and humor and drive that keeps us young, keeps us moving and keeps us smiling.
I love you guys!

And in memory of Andy "Pop" Schmidt
Sparks 4H, Baltimore County.
You taught us all how to have some fun
and learn a little something!

LISA B. KAMPS

Other titles by this author

Emeralds and Gold: A Treasury of Irish Short Stories *(anthology)*
Finding Dr. Right, Silhouette Special Edition
Crossing The Line (The Baltimore Banners, Book 1)
Game Over (The Baltimore Banners, Book 2)
Blue Ribbon Summer (The Baltimore Banners, Book 3)
Time To Heal

LISA B. KAMPS

ONE

Ian Donovan stared at his sister as if she had recently lost her mind. Her hair curled around her face in fiery strands, and her blue eyes threatened to give him frostbite. Her chin lifted with a stubborn jut as she stared him down, and he finally looked away.

His eyes darted to the twins standing uncertainly on either side of her, then to the several suitcases lined up behind them. Ian swallowed and finally looked back at his sister, not quite able to meet her steady gaze.

"Ian, you promised!"

"I know, but--"

"No. No 'buts'. You promised! I told you when you suggested that Danny and I take this trip that we couldn't get anyone to watch the girls for a whole month. I *told* you that! And what did you say?"

"Uh--"

"You said, 'don't worry about it, Bonnie. I'll watch the girls'. Do you remember saying that?"

"Well, yeah, but--"

"And then you went ahead and paid for the trip. Danny took vacation time for this. You cannot weasel your way out of this one."

Ian sucked in his breath and absently rubbed his hand along the back of his neck, still not able to meet Bonnie's eyes. It didn't matter that she was several inches shorter. It didn't matter that she was a few years younger.

She had always bested him, had always been able to stare him down and bend him to her will when they were growing up.

Some things never changed.

Ian let out the breath he had been holding, feeling himself

deflate with the action. A glint came into Bonnie's eyes, letting him know that she realized she had won this one, too. His gaze darted once more to the twins, and he eyed them with suspicion.

He looked up when Bonnie squeezed his arm, her eyes now warm and affectionate. Of course they were--she had gotten what she wanted. Again. Never mind that it had been his suggestion to begin with. How was he supposed to know she was going to take him up on the babysitting offer? Even when he talked to her last night, he had been convinced she wasn't serious. How could she have taken him seriously? He was the carefree, untamed older brother. Of course he hadn't thought she took him seriously--right up until she had called again this morning to let him know they were on their way over.

He eyed the twins again, wondering what they were up to. And they were up to something, he could tell. He wasn't fooled by their innocent looks as they glanced shyly up at him. Oh no, he knew better.

"Ian, are you listening to me?"

He pulled his gaze away from the girls and turned back to his sister, who was now all business as she tried handing him an overstuffed binder.

"Girls, why don't you go into the other room and read while Mommy goes over this stuff with Uncle Ian?" The girls nodded politely and skipped down the hall, leaving the two adults alone. Ian looked after them, wondering what they could be up to, then found himself being pulled down on the sofa next to his sister.

"Everything you need is in here. Phone numbers, contacts, their daily routine. What they like and don't like. And Ian, please, do not turn them into television junkies. We're trying to limit how much TV they watch. They love reading, so take them to the library."

He stared at his sister again. "The library?"

"Yes, the library. And don't forget, they're in FFA now and getting ready for the fair, so you'll have to take them to work with the animals."

"The fair?"

"Yes. It's in four weeks and the girls can't wait. They've been looking forward to it since March. They've worked so hard, learning how to care for the animals. They're really excited about it."

"The animals? You mean like...a dog or something?"

"For crying out loud, Ian. No. Animals. Farm animals. Like cows and chickens and pigs."

"Cows?" Ian stared at the woman next to him, the one who looked exactly like his sister. Only it couldn't be his sister, because she wasn't making any sense. "Cows? In Baltimore City?"

Bonnie let out an impatient sigh and dug through the binder, searching. She pulled out a sheet of paper and nearly threw it at him. "No, Ian. Not in Baltimore. In the county. The animals are at my friend's place in White Hall. The girls have been going up there several times a week since Spring. They've worked really hard, and they're really looking forward to it. So you have to take them up there so they can keep up with it."

"Up there? In White Hall? Where the hell is that?"

"It's up in Maryland Line. Just get on I-83 and keep driving north. And Ian, you have to watch your language. These are my children, not your hockey buddies."

Ian clamped his mouth shut against the string of curses he wanted to utter. Maryland Line? He had no idea where that was, but even he could figure out it must be almost to Pennsylvania. He glanced down at the paper she had shoved into his hand, gave it the briefest glance, and shoved it back in the binder.

"Ian, are you sure you can handle this? Maybe this isn't such a good idea after all." Bonnie's voice hitched and he looked over at her, at the moisture welling in her eyes. Panic seized him at the thought she might start crying and he reached out to awkwardly pat her on the shoulder.

"Bonnie, it'll be fine. Seriously. You and Danny go and enjoy yourselves. The girls will be fine here. Honest."

"Ian, are you sure?"

"Yes, I'm sure." He nudged her playfully like he used to when they were kids. "Hey, you survived growing up with me as a brother, right? And the girls like me--I'm their most favoritest uncle."

"You're their only uncle, you dork."

"Exactly. It'll be fun, and they'll be fine. Don't worry."

She slouched on the sofa next to him, chewing on her lower lip as she watched him, worry still clear in her eyes. Her chest heaved with a heavy sigh and she shook her head, her wild curls bouncing with the movement. "If you're sure..."

"Yes, Bonnie, I'm sure."

"Okay. But remember--they're my girls. They're impressionable. No wild parties, no drinking, no cussing--"

"Christ Bonnie, what kind of guy do you think I am?" He was actually insulted. Did his sister honestly think he was like that?

"I'm sorry. I know you're not like that. It's just...I've seen the stories about how some athletes act and--no, don't get upset." She reached out and grabbed his arm, squeezing. "I know not you and your friends. I know that. But I'm their mother and I'm still going to worry."

Ian sat still, just staring at her, trying to guilt her much like she had guilted him earlier. It didn't work. Of course it didn't--he was missing the necessary chromosome.

Bonnie pushed herself from the sofa and took a few steps toward the door. "Sara, Shelly, come here."

The twins came running down the hall and threw themselves at her, wrapping their arms around her and nearly sending her flying.

"Now you girls behave, and be nice to Uncle Ian, okay?"

"We will, Mom." The two spoke in unison, nodding solemnly. Ian stood off to the side, watching the good-byes and gritting his teeth when he saw Bonnie's eyes tear up. He took a step toward her and playfully nudged her again.

"Hey, they'll be fine. Honest. Now go. You and Danny deserve this." Ian stood, immobile, as Bonnie threw herself into his arms and hugged him tightly. His arms came around her and he hugged her back, surprised at the strong emotion that welled up inside him.

He finally pushed her away and motioned toward the door. "We'll be fine, you'll see. Now go!"

She hugged the girls one last time and offered Ian a small smile and a wave before leaving. The door closed with a soft click that echoed in the suddenly unnatural quiet behind him.

The quiet stretched on for a long minute before being broken by something that sounded suspiciously like a sniffle. Ian stiffened. The sniffle was followed by another one, louder this time, then another. And another.

Ian closed his eyes and took a deep breath, praying he was imagining things. Please let him be imagining things.

He slowly turned and opened his eyes, looking down at the twins. They both stared up at him, tears running down their faces, their thin chests rising and falling with sobs. Ian's stomach clenched in panic and he shook his head.

"No. No crying. Please. You're not supposed to cry."

"We want Mommy!" Sara whimpered. Or maybe it was Shelly. Hell, he couldn't tell, not with them dressed do much alike.

And then it didn't matter, because the whimpering started in earnest, identical tears and identical wails coming from identical twins that looked exactly like their mother.

Ian sat down on the floor and dropped his head into his hands, suddenly feeling like crying himself.

#

Forty-eight hours later, Ian was sorely tempted to tie the twins together with rope, throw them into the trunk of his car, and leave them in the airport parking lot while he took off for destination unknown.

Loud squeals echoed through the house, the pitch set at the perfect decibel needed to shatter his eardrums. He flinched as the sound pierced his ears and bounced around inside his head, then groaned and reached for another pillow to pull over his head. He didn't know what time it was, and he didn't care. He just wanted sleep. Sweet, blissful, quiet sleep.

His bedroom door flew open, crashing against the wall with a bang loud enough to let him know that there was now a hole in the drywall. He swallowed a groan and held the pillows tighter over his head, briefly wondering if it was possible to smother himself.

All fantasies of escape disappeared as his bed dipped under the weight of the two girls. And dipped. And dipped some more as they jumped up and down, their giggling bouncing around the room until it found the base of his skull and pressed against him painfully.

"Uncle Ian, Uncle Ian, Uncle Ian!"

"Get up, get up, get up!"

Ian groaned, still clutching the pillows tightly over his head. Small hands grabbed his and pulled, and the pillows went flying. His eyes opened to slits to see the muted gray light of dawn filtering into his bedroom, and he groaned more loudly.

"She-devils! You're both she-devils!" Ian's bellow went unnoticed by both girls, who continued to jump up and down. One of them came dangerously close to landing in a very sensitive spot and he rolled away, instinctively cupping himself under the covers just in time.

Part of him wanted to cry. He just wanted to roll over, beg mercy, and break down into tears. How the hell did his sister do this every single day, on top of working?

"Enough!"

Both girls ended their jumping with athletic belly flops that had them landing on either side of him. He closed his eyes and let his head fall back, savoring the brief silence.

"Uncle Ian, what's wrong?"

He peeled open one eye to see two sets of identical blue eyes staring back at him in wide-eyed innocence. Ha! He knew better.

"She-devils," he growled again. Giggles greeted his declaration and he sighed in defeat. They were only seven, but already they knew exactly which buttons to push.

Just like their mother.

"Uncle Ian, did you forget?"

"We got to go work with the animals today."

"We're ready to go."

"You need to take us."

The rapid-fire back-and-forth between the two girls was enough to leave him feeling like he was listening to a ping-pong match. He groaned again and lifted his arm, bringing it close to his face so he could squint at his watch.

6:12.

In the morning.

It was the off-season. He should still be sleeping. Instead, he had exactly four hours of sleep.

And the girls didn't need to be there until ten.

He groaned again and wiped his hands across his face, rubbing his eyes, trying to wake himself from this nightmare. Knowing it was hopeless, he pushed himself up on his elbows and glared at the two girls.

"Out! Go downstairs and, I don't know, make breakfast or something. I'll be down in a minute."

They bounced off the bed and tore out of his room, leaving blissful silence in their wake. Ian thought about just closing his eyes and going back to sleep. Just for another hour. Hell, just for another fifteen minutes. That was all he needed--

A crash from the kitchen catapulted him from bed. He stumbled through the door, not even trying to guess what havoc had been wreaked.

"She-devils."

TWO

Kayli Evans hummed along with the country music blaring from the radio, dumping the feed into a bucket then walking over to the water trough. She turned the faucet off then rolled up the water hose, dragging it back to the barn. The only thing left to do this morning was take a round bale down to the field.

Then get ready for the twins and help them get ready for the fair.

She glanced at her watch. It was barely eight-thirty, plenty of time left. She brushed at the streak of mud on the side of her leg then yanked the gloves from her back pocket.

"Hey Lori!" She poked her head into the chicken house attached to the barn and spied her niece teasing one of the barn cats with a piece of straw. The girl glanced up, a look of guilt on her face. Kayli rolled her eyes but didn't say anything. "Tell your dad I'm taking a round bale down, will you?"

"Okay, yeah."

"And Lori? Don't forget about the chickens, okay? I'm really counting on you to help out."

A heavy sigh followed Kayli out the door, and she bit back her grin. She, more than anyone else, understood Lori's frustration at having to work on such a gorgeous summer day. And she knew that it wasn't easy for any fourteen-year-old girl to give up part of every summer day to work on a small farm--not when she should be spending all of those days with her father.

Thankfully, Lori adjusted well, and was proving to be more than helpful. Kayli made a mental note to tell her that later tonight, when everyone had a chance to sit down and relax.

She walked around the side of the huge barn and pulled open the heavy door, standing in the entranceway until her eyes adjusted to the dim interior light. She climbed up onto the old Farmall and pushed the button, sending up a small prayer of thanks when the engine cranked over with a loud rumble.

Kayli had the round bale loaded and was backing out of the barn when the sound of a horn caused her to jump. The blaring continued, loud and insistent, and she slammed the tractor to a stop before turning around in the seat to see what was going on.

She blinked several times, having trouble believing her eyes. The rear tractor tire was less than two feet away from the hood of a shiny black convertible. An expensive shiny black convertible.

Muttering under her breath, she jumped down from the tractor and walked around to the rear, ready to yell at whoever was stupid enough to drive up on private property and pull in front of a barn.

Her mouth closed with a snap and her heart thundered in her chest when she saw a dark head leaning over the steering wheel. For a brief second she wondered if the tractor had somehow hit the car, if the man driving had somehow been injured. But then she noticed the two young girls bouncing in the back seat, laughter lighting their faces. She recognized them immediately, and felt a welcoming smile spread across her face.

"Hey Sara, Shelly. How's it going?"

The girls unfastened their seat belts and climbed over the side of the car, paying no attention whatsoever to the paint as they jumped out and ran over to her. They gave her a quick hug, then fired questions at her so fast she had trouble understanding them.

Kayli finally laughed and shook her head, holding her hand up to stop them. She had never seen them so wound up before. "Whoa, hold it! Slow down. What has gotten into you two?"

With choreographed precision, both girls immediately stopped talking and stood up straighter, the picture of well-behaved innocence. Kayli looked at them with raised eyebrows, again wondering what had gotten into them.

"Can we go see the chickens?"

"Please?"

She watched them for a minute longer then offered them a smile and pointed behind her. "Go ahead. Lori could use the help collecting the eggs. But be careful!" She called after them, wondering if they even heard her as they took off at a run around the barn.

"How did you do that?"

Kayli started at the deep voice and slowly turned, suddenly remembering the man driving. Dark piercing eyes met hers and she had to stop herself from taking a step back at their intensity.

The man's eyes weren't the only thing that was intense. His whole presence was intense...and he was still sitting behind the wheel. If the rest of him looked anything like what she could see...

His dark shaggy hair was windblown, swept back from a high forehead. His face was all square angles: high cheekbones, sculpted jaw, and a generous full mouth. A neatly clipped van dyke beard and mustache framed the entire package, making him look even more delectable.

And dangerous. Like an eighteenth century rake bent on debauchery. If not for the bewildered look on his face, Kayli may have felt threatened.

Instead, she felt...intrigued. And just a little bit curious.

"I'm sorry. Excuse me?"

The man shook his head, almost as if he was trying to clear it, then pushed open the door and stepped out of the low-riding sports car. A BMW, now that Kayli looked closer at it. What kind of idiot drove a BMW uphill along a rutted drive?

The man stepped around the front of the car toward her and Kayli had to force herself not to look him up and down. Apparently the same kind of idiot who wore dark slacks, a tailored polo shirt, and expensive leather loafers while driving the aforementioned BMW. And yes, he may be an idiot, but he was a tall, muscular, well-dressed idiot. And gorgeous. Yeah, the idiot was drop-dead gorgeous.

And so out of place she had to bite her lip to keep from laughing. Especially when he motioned after the girls with a bewildered look on his face.

"How did you do that?"

"I'm sorry, I'm not sure--"

"The she-devils. How did you get them to listen to you?"

Kayli frowned and looked behind her, wondering who he was talking about. She shook her head and took a hesitant step back. "The she-devils?"

"Yeah. The twins. Sara and Shelly. They haven't stopped going since Bonnie and Danny left on vacation." He turned his gaze back to her, his eyes clearing as he finally looked at her. Kayli's stomach did a little roll at all that intensity focused on her and again almost took a step backward at the look in his eyes.

Realization of who this must be dawned on her just as he stepped forward and offered her his hand, a grin splitting his face and dancing in his eyes. "Sorry. I should probably introduce myself. Ian Donovan, the she-devils' uncle."

"Kayli Evans." She pulled her gloves off and wiped her hand on her shorts before shaking his hand. His grasp was firm, warm...and sent a jolt of awareness shooting up her arm before he released his hold on her.

So this was Bonnie's famous hockey player brother. Well, at least now she understood the car and the clothes. But not why he was here.

"Um, is there something I can help you with, Mr. Donovan?"

His grin faded, losing a bit of its wattage as he looked at her then motioned around them. "Bonnie said something about the girls and animals. I just came to drop them off. I'm sorry if we're a little early but they were pretty excited and...what's wrong?"

She apparently hadn't done a very good job of hiding her smile or swallowing her chuckle, because he was now looking at her with something that almost looked like fear in his eyes. Kayli looked away and cleared her throat, then turned back to him, doing her best to keep the smile from her face.

"The early part isn't a big problem. But I'm afraid there was some misunderstanding about everything else."

"Misunderstanding?"

"Um, yeah. First, we don't work with the animals here. I mean, we do, but down the road. You missed the driveway about a quarter mile back."

"I did?"

"Yeah. That one's actually paved, and not quite as steep." Again Kayli bit back her smile, trying not to laugh when he turned back to his car with such a forlorn expression on his face that she almost felt sorry for him. She couldn't even begin to imagine how many times the sleek Beemer must have bottomed out coming up the gravel drive to the barn.

He turned back toward her, the laughter in his eyes all but gone by now, replaced by something that looked very much like dread. "You said 'first'. I'm guessing that means there's a 'second'?"

This time Kayli did laugh. She couldn't help it, not with the expression on his face. Thankfully he didn't seem to mind, just waited with one brow raised, as if he was expecting the worst. "Yeah, there's a 'second'. This isn't a drop-off kind of thing. The girls need to have an adult with them to help out with the animals."

"Help? With the animals?"

"Yeah." Kayli paused, eyeing him with even more curiosity. "Didn't Bonnie explain what this was for?"

Ian glanced up toward the sky, as if he was seeking answers to silent questions before looking at her and shaking his head. "Well, I thought she did. But I'm beginning to think she left out a few things."

An expectant silence stretched between them and Kayli almost felt sorry for him, but was still unable to hide her smile. "The girls will be getting their cattle ready for showing at the fair. But you need to stay and help, because you'll be showing with them."

#

Ian ended the call then slipped the cell phone back into his pocket. He was at a complete loss on where to go from here, now that his golf game was cancelled and going home was out of the question.

He threw one last longing look at his car, trying not to wince at all the mud, dust, and...shit. A dent. He squinted and looked closer. Damn, it was definitely a dent, right there at the bottom of the passenger door. Of course there would be a dent--he had just bought the damn car not even two months ago. It figured.

At least it hadn't been flattened by the tractor backing out of the barn.

He leaned down closer and ran his hand along the door. Maybe he could take it into the shop and they could--

Ian straightened at the sound of a loud engine coming from behind him, and all thoughts of dents and body shops left him as he watched a huge ATV slide to a stop in front of him. Well, maybe there was a thought or two of body shops, but not the kind that had anything to do with cars.

He watched as Kayli cut the motor of the four-wheeler and just stared at him, her hazel eyes clear, bold, and assessing. Ian was grateful that she couldn't see his own eyes behind the dark lenses of his sunglasses, because he was certain she would have slapped him if she could.

Who would have ever thought that seeing a woman straddle a four-wheeler could be a turn-on? Although maybe that wasn't such an odd thing, not when the woman looked like Kayli.

She was shorter than he was, about five-ten, which would put the top of her head right about to his chin. Perfect, as far as he was concerned. And she was blessed with just the right amount of curves in just the right places. Those same curves filled out the soft denim of her shorts and pushed against the cotton of the tank shirt she was wearing beneath an open short-sleeve work shirt.

The clunky, dusty work boots he could have done without but, somehow, they worked with the outfit.

Probably because she was working.

He watched as she reached up and tucked a wayward strand of honey-colored hair behind her ear, mesmerized at the fluid movement. Then he found himself staring at her lips, full and sensuous, tilting up at the corners in a small smile.

"Mr. Donovan!"

Ian gave himself a small shake, realizing she had been talking to him while he had been staring. No, he amended, while he had been caught staring. He cleared his throat and focused his gaze over Kayli's shoulder, concentrating on the weathered siding of the barn behind her.

"Mr. Donovan, would you like to follow me back, or do you think you can find it okay on your own?"

It took a full minute before he could make sense of her words, a full minute that left him feeling like a dimwit. She was talking about driving back to the main house, where the she-devils were already heading.

For play time with farm animals.

He was going to have such a long talk with his sister when she got back.

Ian glanced back toward the rutted, washed out driveway he had bounced up earlier. He did his best not to shudder at the thought of going back down the same way, wondering if the car could handle the return trip without further damage. But it wasn't like he had much choice.

He also didn't remember seeing any other driveway on his way up. "Maybe I should follow you. I'm not sure where I'm going and--"

Kayli started the four-wheeler with a grin, revving the throttle to somewhere just below a loud roar. Ian took that as his signal to leave, and quickly climbed into the car and started it up. His teeth jarred in his mouth as he turned the M3 around and followed her down the driveway, each bump and dip a physical blow.

The one good thing about following the four-wheeler down was that he couldn't really hear the scrape and grind of the undercarriage as it hit.

And, yeah, Kayli's rear view as she straddled the behemoth ATV helped improve his outlook as well.

He followed her down to the road, and sure enough, there was another driveway on his left. And yes, thank God, this one was paved. Kayli turned into it, pausing to wait for him, then motioned ahead of her, pointing to a shaded area large enough for several cars to park. He waved to indicate he understood, then watched in appreciation as she kicked the monster into gear and took off, shooting across the driveway and into a field toward several smaller outbuildings.

Ian maneuvered the car into the shaded area then cut the engine and got out, his gaze drawn to the large Victorian farmhouse further up the drive. Freshly painted with dainty trim and a round turret and a full wrap-around porch complete with a swing, the house sat quietly amid several large willow trees and a fully grown garden exploding with color.

Ian could imagine himself sitting on the porch swing, sipping a beer as Kayli curled up next to him with her luscious curves and...

Where the hell had that thought come from? Too much country air already, probably. He shook his head and smiled to himself, heading toward the house that beckoned invitingly. Maybe this whole adventure wouldn't be so bad after all, he thought.

He was less than ten feet away from the house, walking along the uneven cobbled stones when he heard a shout. A dark blur flashed in his peripheral vision a split-second before he felt something slam into his legs. The unexpected contact threw him off-balance, one foot catching in the uneven walkway. His arms pin wheeled for balance but it was too late and he went down, rolling under the ball of fur that was now on top of him.

The mingled scents of dog breath and farm assaulted him as he threw his arms up, trying to stop the slobbering beast from drooling all over him.

"Ronan! Down!" The sharply-spoken command brought the dog to a halt, and Ian pushed himself up on his elbows, expecting to come face-to-face with a furry behemoth.

Instead, he was eye-to-eye with a smiling border collie, its shaggy black and white tail waving frantically. Ian looked up to see Kayli coming to a stop, her cheeks flushed from running toward him. She leaned down and pointed her finger at the dog, giving Ian a nice view of tanned, firm skin. All he had to do was shift just a little more--

"Bad boy!"

Ian jumped, thinking he had been caught trying to stare down her shirt, then realized Kayli was talking to the dog. He let out a soft sigh and adjusted his gaze to safer scenery, like her boots.

"I am so sorry," Kaylie apologized. Ian took the hand she offered and gripped it firmly, not because he needed help standing, but because he just wanted to touch her again. But he probably should have let go sooner, because she flashed him an indecipherable look as she pulled her hand away and stepped back.

"I have no idea why he did that. He's usually better behaved." She glanced down at the dog, then back at Ian, her gaze raking over him as a frown creased her brow. "And now he's got dirt and everything all over you. I am so sorry."

Ian looked down at himself, not surprised to see muddy paw prints and streaks of dirt over his shirt and pants. What did surprise him was when Kayli reached out, her brow furrowed in concentration, and began brushing the dirt from his pants legs like he was a two-year old who didn't know how to stay clean. Ian stepped back, surprised not only by her touch but by his body's swift reaction to that same touch.

But Kayli didn't seem to notice. She was still bent over in front of him as she drew one hand to her face and sniffed. Ian took another step back just as he heard a screen door bang open and shut behind him.

And great, here came Luke Duke's twin down the steps, looking like he would be more than happy to kick Ian's ass. Was it her boyfriend? Husband? Ian hadn't noticed a ring but that didn't mean anything. He took another step back just as Kayli turned toward the dog, the murderous look on her face at odds with the sparkle in her eyes.

The boyfriend/husband came to a stop at the bottom of the porch steps and surveyed the scene with a cool detachment. "Kayli, what is going on out here?"

"Your dog! Dammit Ronan, when are you going to stop rolling in cow shit?"

THREE

Flecks of light glittered in the closing darkness, blinking in time to the cricket song that echoed in the still air. Kayli pushed her toe against the porch and set the swing in motion, adding a rhythmic creak to the soft background noise. She rested her head against the back of the swing and closed her eyes with a soft sigh.

This was her favorite time of day, when day and night hovered together in the odd light of twilight and made it seem as if time stood still, if only for a few minutes. It was the one time of the day when everything slowed then stopped, when anything was possible, when nothing mattered.

A chance just to be.

The screen door opened and closed with a soft creak. The sound of booted footsteps headed in her direction, stopping in front of her. She sighed again and opened her eyes to see Jake leaning against the porch railing, his strong profile shadowed in the darkening light as he stared across the front yard. He must have sensed her watching him because he turned toward her, a small grin on his face as held out a bottle of beer for her. She leaned forward to take it, then took a long swallow before sitting back.

"So how did today go?"

Kayli shrugged, then rolled her neck and shoulders to work out some of the kinks. "I suppose okay. The twins are catching on quick. And everyone had fun, so...Who knows? If this works out, maybe I'll start a summer camp." She let her words drift away with another shrug, staring past Jake into the deepening night.

Jake watched her for a quiet minute then hoisted himself onto the porch railing, balancing himself against the newly-painted column. "What? Why? I thought you were just helping the girls get ready for the fair."

"Yeah, but I was thinking that if this worked, I could really start a camp, maybe get some more money coming in. It wouldn't hurt." Silence greeted her statement, as she knew it would. Just as she knew that she had now opened a topic of conversation that was better left alone, at least as far as she was concerned.

"Speaking of that--"

"Jake, please, not right now."

"We need to talk about it sooner or later. And with me due to ship back out, we're running out of time."

"No, we're not. Everything is fine." *For now.* But she knew better than to say those words out loud.

Jake leaned his head against the porch column and took a long drink from his own bottle. Kayli watched him in the shadows, and could see his jaw clench even from where she sat. She pushed herself up from the swing and went to stand next to him, leaning against the railing so she was close to him, but so that she wouldn't have to look at him.

"Kayli, something needs to be done. You know that. You can't keep doing it by yourself. You deserve a real life. With me gone--"

She turned toward him and met his gaze, not even trying to hide the pleading in her own eyes. "Not tonight. Okay? Can't we just sit here and relax? Please?"

He kept watching her, his own gaze steady and serious. The seconds ticked around them, each one longer as she held her breath and waited. Jake finally looked away with a loud sigh and shook his head, and she knew she had won this one small round.

But she knew her time for winning was running out, and that Jake was right. Sooner or later, before he left, they were going to have to talk about their options.

Talk about hiring help they couldn't afford...or talk about their brother Cole coming back.

Kayli's stomach churned at the last thought but she ruthlessly pushed it away. Now was *not* the time to talk about it. Or even think about it. She turned away from Jake and hoisted herself up on the porch railing, swinging her feet against the spindles with a soft tap-tap-tap. Several minutes went by before Jake reached out and nudged her leg with the toe of his boot.

"Stop it. God, now I know why Mom always yelled at you for doing that. It's annoying."

Kayli resisted the urge to stick her tongue out at him, but just barely. She had succeeded in getting Jake's mind onto something else, which is what she had set out to do. She didn't want to push her luck with anything else.

"So...I think Mr. Hockey has the hots for you."

The statement, made so casually in the deepening darkness, was so unexpected that Kayli nearly fell off the railing. She tightened her grip on both the wood pillar and her beer bottle and shot Jake a look of such disbelief that he actually laughed at her.

"Oh, please."

"I'm serious. He kept staring at you all day. I thought I was going to have to go all big brother on him."

A blush heated her face. Kayli lifted the bottle to her lips and drank deeply, hoping Jake wouldn't be able to see it. Yes, she had noticed Ian staring at her with those darkly intense eyes--because she had been doing her best not to stare at him. And her staring had nothing to do with how out of place he had been, with his fancy sports car and fancy clothes.

He was so different from what she had expected, so different from her down-to-earth and funny friend Bonnie that she still couldn't believe the two were related.

"I don't think you have to worry about that. I'm not exactly in the same league with him, you know." Kayli had meant the words as a light-hearted tease, but even she was surprised by the wistful defeat she heard in her voice. Wistful or not, though, it was the truth. Ian Donovan lived on a level so far out of her realm of experience that they may have come from two different galaxies.

"Really? So who do you think is in your league? And please don't even think of saying Cody Miller."

Kayli whipped her head around and made phony gagging noises. She had gone out with him on exactly two dates, and the second one was only because she thought the first one was a fluke and that he really couldn't be that bad.

She had been wrong.

"Uh, no. Eww. No Cody Miller. No thanks."

"Glad to hear you have some sense, anyway. But I don't get why you're saying you're not in the same league as Mr. Hockey."

"You're joking, right? Did you see that car he was driving? I mean, what's something like that cost? Fifty thousand? And his clothes. I mean, really. Who even dresses like that up here?"

"Actually, that Beemer probably runs closer to a hundred grand. And he had planned on dropping off the twins then going golfing, which is why he was dressed like that."

Kayli opened her mouth but no sound came out. She was still so stuck on the fact that some people actually paid that much money for a car that she couldn't think of a single sarcastic remark about dressing up to play golf. Jake either didn't see her struggle, or chose to ignore it because he kept on talking.

"Trust me. Mr. Hockey has the hots for you. You should go out with him when he asks."

Kayli ignored the little thrill that shot through her at the idea of being asked out but she pushed it away as she dropped down from the railing and handed Jake her empty bottle. Now was not the time for unrealistic day dreams.

"He does not have the hots for me, and he's not going to ask me out. And if he did, I would say no. We don't have anything in common, and I'm not interested, anyway." She walked across the porch and went inside, letting the screen door slam shut but not before she caught her brother's last laughing word.

"Liar."

#

"Great job, Shelly. Just remember to grip the halter closer to her head, and keep that head up. Sara, try not to look down too much-- you want to keep your eyes up and look at the judge all the time, okay?" Kayli clasped both girls on the shoulder then took the leads from their hands, taking control of the cattle. She motioned over her shoulder. "Why don't you guys go hang with Lori a little bit, okay?"

The twins nodded then took off at a run across the field. Kayli shook her head at their enthusiasm then turned the cattle and headed into the small barn. The cool dimness was a welcome respite after being in the hot sun, and she breathed in deeply of the cool air and mingled barn scents.

She led the heifers into the double stall and removed their halters, then tossed a few flakes of hay in the corner before closing the gate. Kayli leaned her arms along the top of the railing and watched them eat, smiling when one of them broke away and came over to nose her hand. She laughed and rubbed her palm up and down between the heifer's eyes.

"Did you need any help with them?"

The quiet inquiry startled her and she whirled around in surprise to see Ian silhouetted in the doorway. He took a step toward her then stopped, and she could see the grin on his face even from where she was standing.

"Sorry, I didn't mean to surprise you. I just thought you might need some help."

Kayli pulled her gaze away and walked toward a water barrel in the corner then dunked both her hands in and swirled them around. She shook them off then wiped them against her shorts, taking care not to look over at him when she answered. "Nope, I'm good. But thanks anyway."

Kayli expected him to turn around and leave, but he didn't. In fact, he took a few more steps into the barn and looked around before he leaned against the stone wall, one foot crossed in front of the other. She glanced down at his feet and noticed he still wore some kind of expensive loafer, and tried not to smile. "It feels good in here. I didn't think a barn would be so cool."

"Um, yeah. It helps that this part of it is kinda underground, plus the stone and..." Kayli let her voice fade away, realizing that she was starting to ramble. She seriously doubted if Ian was interested in why the place was cool, and was probably only making conversation. Why he would do that, she didn't know. "Anyway, we're done for the day, so you don't have to hang around anymore. Sara and Shelly can go home now."

Ian didn't say anything, just watched her from where he was standing, that small grin still on his face. Kayli turned away, more than just a little unnerved, and searched for something to do. Any other time there would be at least a dozen little projects that would keep her occupied. Today, she couldn't find anything. Her eyes drifted to the hay bales stacked in the corner, and she headed toward them, deciding to move them closer to the stalls.

Just for something to do. Because she couldn't just stand here and do nothing, not while Ian watched her with those intense eyes and that unnerving grin.

She grabbed one of the bales by the twine and turned, then almost walked straight into Ian with it. He stepped back just in time, still smiling at her. Kayli shook her head and moved past him without a word, then placed the bale against the wall where he had been leaning. She turned to get another one and stopped in surprise.

Ian had grabbed a second bale and was now walking toward her with it. He raised his brows and nodded toward the first bale. "Do you want this on top of that one?"

Kayli reached out to take it from him, surprised even more when he side-stepped her and set the bale down. "Mr. Donovan, I appreciate it but I really don't need--"

"It's Ian."

"Whatever. Listen, I appreciate it but I really don't need your help so--"

"I don't mind."

"No, really. Thanks but..." She waved her hands in front of him, motioning to his clothes. He was dressed in khaki linen trousers and a loose-fitting buttoned shirt that looked more appropriate for boating than hauling hay bales. "You're really not dressed for it and we wouldn't want you to get your clothes all dirty. So thanks, but I got it."

Ian's grin faded a bit with her biting comment, and she thought there was a flash of something in his dark eyes--irritation, maybe?--but she ignored it as she went to get another bale. Her last comment had come out sharper than she had meant it to, and she knew she should probably apologize, but she was too hot and irritated to fall back on good manners. And unnerved. What was it about Bonnie's brother that made her so...nervous? And jumpy.

The conversation with Jake from two nights ago came back, as clear as if it had just happened.

Probably because she couldn't forget it. And every time she remembered it, she became more irritated.

With Jake, for putting foolish thoughts in her head.

With herself, for just thinking those foolish thoughts.

She heaved the bale and turned, and this time she really did walk straight into Ian, with enough force to send him stumbling back a few steps. Kayli bit down on the retort that sprang to mind, and nimbly stepped around him. She expected him to say something but he didn't, he just picked up the fourth bale and fixed her with a look she didn't really understand. He tossed it on top of the pile and kept looking at her.

"And again, I really don't mind. I've been dirty before. Do you need the others moved?" He kept her pinned with that unreadable look, long enough to make her feel uncomfortable...or like he was waiting for an apology. So she took a step back and let out a sigh, wondering what had gotten into her, wondering why she was being so rude. She tried to smile, or at least not frown so much.

"No, that's it. Thank you. Um, like I said before, we're done here so--"

A chorus of screeching mixed with giggles interrupted her, and Kayli hurried to the door to see what was going on. She was nearly run over by the twins racing into the barn, followed by a laughing Lori.

"Uncle Ian, can we?"

"Please Uncle Ian?"

Kayli turned to see both girls jumping up and down in front of their uncle, their wild curls bouncing around identical faces as they looked up at him with pleading eyes. Ian looked from one upturned face to the other, bewilderment clear in his eyes.

"Can you what?"

"Can we go?"

"Lori said she'd take us!"

Kayli turned toward her niece, her own eyes silently questioning the young girl. Lori shrugged, still laughing.

"I just asked if they wanted to go down to the pond and feed the ducks, that's all. I didn't think they'd go all nuts about it."

Kayli bit back the smile she felt trying to break free. Feeding ducks wouldn't have been at the top of her list for excitement, but she wasn't a seven-year-old girl who didn't get to see ducks very often. She glanced over at the trio, at the girls still silently pleading with their uncle, then at Ian, who looked so lost that he had no idea what to say or do.

No, she didn't want to invite him to stay, not when his presence did nothing but throw her off-track and make her skittish and uncomfortable and a bunch of other different things she didn't want to acknowledge. But that was her problem, nobody else's, and it wasn't fair to disappoint the two young girls just because their uncle made her feel uncomfortable.

Besides, she could find plenty of errands to do that would keep her away from Ian Donovan.

"It's no big deal. You guys can stay if you want. Lori can take all of you down to look." She turned back to her niece. "Why don't you grab something to drink and a few snacks to take down with you, and the four of you can have a quick picnic and watch the ducks. I have to run to Lineboro to pick up some feed, anyway."

"Oh, Uncle Ian can't come."

"Nope, he can't. That'll ruin it."

Kayli's hopes for a clean escape were dashed by the solemn looks on the girls' faces, and by Lori's smothered laughter. She gave her niece a questioning look.

"Um, we were going to look for frogs while we were down there."

"To find Prince Charming."

"So we can be princesses."

Kayli closed her eyes and silently counted to ten while her mind worked to come up with alternate plans. Just because the girls didn't want Ian to go with them didn't mean he couldn't.

She opened her eyes to say as much but her mouth snapped closed. The twins were staring at their uncle with wide moist eyes, looking their hearts would be broken if he said they couldn't go without him.

Ian was looking back at them with such a lost, bewildered expression that Kayli knew, probably even before he did, that he was going to give in without even the smallest of fights. And as much as she didn't want it to, her heart melted the tiniest bit when she realized that he was a complete and total push-over when it came to his nieces.

The offer came tumbling out of her mouth before she could stop and think about what she was doing.

"Well then, I guess Uncle Ian can come with me to the feed store."

FOUR

Ian shifted again on the hard bench seat, knowing that the chances of him getting comfortable had flown out the open window of the beat up Ford as soon as they pulled out of the driveway. But he wasn't shifting to get comfortable; he was shifting so he could watch Kayli out of the corner of his eye.

She sat in the driver's seat, guiding the pick-up along narrow country roads as if she could do it with her eyes closed. A few strands of her long hair whipped around her face, pulled free from her pony tail by work and the wind. Her left arm rested carelessly on the doorframe, her fingers tapping out the beat of the country music that filled the cab while her right hand curled loosely around the steering wheel.

She hadn't changed before they left, and was still wearing what he had dubbed her work clothes: worn denim cut-offs, a short-sleeve shirt opened over a gray tank shirt, and dusty work boots. He wondered if she ever wore anything else, wondered what she would look like with her hair down, dressed in a slinky black dress. He'd bet a year's salary that four-inch heels would catapult her tanned, toned legs straight beyond the killer category.

Then he wondered what she would look like wearing nothing *but* those four-inch heels, and nearly groaned out loud. He had to do something to keep his mind from wondering things that would only get him into trouble, but conversation was definitely out. He had already tried, and failed miserably.

Where is it we're going?

The feed store.
Have you lived here your whole life?
Yeah.
So, what do you in your spare time?
Sleep.
How far is it?
Not far.
Are we still in Maryland?

That one had gotten him such a look of amused disbelief that he actually leaned over and turned the radio up so he wouldn't ask anymore stupid questions. Because yes, apparently they were still in Maryland and what kind of idiot was he that he wouldn't know that?

Apparently an idiot of the worst kind. But how was he supposed to know? Unlike Kayli, he hadn't grown up here. Yes, he knew Baltimore. And if he stretched it, he could pretend to be familiar with some of the outskirts of Baltimore, but that was about it.

He searched his mind for something to say, but came up blank. Unless he decided to ask her point-blank why she didn't like him. He had picked up on that pretty quickly when she had made the comment about him getting dirty.

He glanced over at her, noticed how relaxed and at-ease she seemed, and he wondered if she had forgotten about him sitting here. That thought made him uncomfortable and irritated enough that he leaned over and turned the radio down once more, which earned him another slightly amused look from Kayli.

"Did I do something for you not to like me, or do you just not like me on general principle?"

Kayli raised one perfect eyebrow at him then turned her attention back to the winding road. "I never said I didn't like you."

"Not in so many words, no."

"Not in any words."

He opened his mouth to say something, then quickly shut it when he realized he had nothing to say back. How was he supposed to reply to that without sounding like an idiot--again? Well, no, you didn't say it, but I have this feeling you don't like me.

Yeah, that would work real well--if he was thirteen-year-old girl.

Ian turned to look back out the window and noticed they were entering a quaint little neighborhood. Or maybe it was a village. Whatever it was called, it looked like something straight out of a fifties television sitcom, provided someone had forgotten to give the set a fresh coat of paint. His teeth jarred when the truck bounced into a rutted lot and came to a stop in front of a rundown building with a dusty loading dock off to one side. Kayli turned the truck around then backed it up to the dock in an expertly smooth move that actually impressed him. He was going to compliment her on her driving skills but she opened the door and jumped down so quickly that he barely heard her muttered command, "Stay here."

And he did. For about thirty seconds before he realized what he was doing. Ian shook his head, not believing he had just been ordered to stay put, then climbed out of the truck and walked toward the door he had seen Kayli disappear into.

The inside of the shop wasn't much better than the outside. The front room was maybe eight feet wide, and five feet deep. A long counter ran along the back, and two glass-front refrigerators stood side-by-side along the outside wall. Racks with chips and jerky and who knew what else hung along the inside wall, and a bulletin board overflowing with notices and fliers of all kinds took up the back wall behind the counter.

Kayli was leaning against the counter, talking to an older man and smiling at something he said. Ian's gaze dipped appreciatively to take in her denim-clad bottom, until he noticed the odd silence surrounding him. His gaze jerked back up and he saw that both Kayli and the older man were staring at him. From the look on the older man's weathered face, Ian knew he had been caught--and found guilty of an unforgivable crime.

Ian cleared his throat and was getting ready to apologize when Kayli turned back around, effectively dismissing him. She was rattling off a verbal list that made no sense to him, but apparently did to the older man because he nodded and made some kind of marks on a worn sheet of paper. Ian watched as the man tallied everything up then wrote up a bill of sale and passed it to Kayli. She glanced at it, scrawled her name on the bottom, then took the copy the man had given her.

"I'll have Billy start pulling it for you."

"Thanks Mr. Johnson." Kayli folded the sheet of paper and tucked it into her back pocket, then turned and walked past Ian without so much as a glance. He stayed where he was, momentarily rooted to the spot, then quickly turned and walked out.

Kayli was already back at the truck, and he watched as she lowered the tailgate then climbed in with a small bounce and jump. She continued ignoring him, so he walked over just as some guy wheeled a pallet of large bags out onto the dock. The guy looked at him with the same expression as the old man had, and Ian wondered what was so wrong with him that everyone glared at him with distrust in their eyes.

"Hey Kayli, how's it going?"

"Same as always, Billy. How's your pop? He looked a little pale when I saw him inside but I didn't want to say anything."

"You know Pop." Billy shrugged, a gesture that could have meant anything but that Kayli obviously understood. She nodded and reached for the bag that Billy held out to her, carelessly tossing it over her shoulder and moving it to the front of the truck bed. Ian watched as she went to reach for the second bag, but Billy held it away from her, his gaze now fixed steadily on Ian.

"Your friend gonna help you with these?"

The question may have been directed at Kayli, but there was no mistaking the accusation aimed at Ian. And wasn't he an idiot for standing here watching instead of offering to help? He moved forward, intent on helping, but stopped short at Kayli's next words.

"Nah, he just came to keep me company on the ride. And he's not really dressed for working." She laughed when she said it, a small musical sound that did nothing to lessen the sting of her words. Ian gritted his teeth and closed the distance between the truck and him, then quickly jumped into the back, his foot sliding only the smallest bit against the dirt and straw and whatever other loose stuff was strewn across the dirty bed. He gave Kayli a short impatient look then reached for the bag that Billy was still holding out.

And promptly dropped it when Billy released his hold on it. Holy shit, the thing was heavier than it looked. Not so heavy that he should have dropped it, but he hadn't expected the weight. He leaned down to pick it back up, impatiently shoving Kayli's hands away when she reached for it.

"No, I've got it."

"But I don't want you to hurt yourself."

He threw the bag over his shoulder, ignoring the pull in his upper back, and shot her a glare. "I said, I've got it."

She stepped back, her hands held in front of her in a

surrendering gesture, and laughed. "If you say so." And then, as if her words and the laughter weren't bad enough for his suddenly bruised ego, she leaned forward and grabbed another bag, tossing it over her shoulder as if it weighed nothing before carrying it to the front of the truck and tossing it down. "Just don't blame me when you ruin your clothes and hurt yourself."

#

Ian couldn't move. He was certain that if he tried, if he concentrated really hard and tried, he could get some part of his body to work.

He didn't want to try.

The mere *thought* of trying hurt.

But the sheer embarrassment of this afternoon hurt worse, so he forced himself to roll over and pushed himself up to a sitting position. Or mostly sitting.

He blew out a deep breath and glanced over at the twins. They were curled up next to each other, sound asleep in his bed. And he really, really needed to wake them up and get them to take a bath, because they were filthy.

And they stank.

Or maybe he was the one who stunk. He looked down at his own clothes and sniffed. It was hard to say, considering all three of them were dirty.

The twins were covered in dried mud, their outfits stiff with dry pond water. They had successfully fed the ducks and searched for frogs--by climbing into the pond and digging along its muddy banks.

He, on the other hand, was covered in dried sweat. Feed dust and dirt and he didn't want to think what else caked his skin and covered his clothes, and he reeked of...eau de farm. And it wasn't a pleasant outdoor smell, either.

He pushed himself to a full sitting position and groaned as a spasm twitched in his back. Just a little one, nothing a quick massage wouldn't fix. Unfortunately for him, there was no chance of a massage in his immediate future. A soak in the Jacuzzi would work, too--if he could find the energy to drag his ass out of the bed and get moving.

He compiled a mental list: wake up the twins and get them

cleaned and into bed.

Burn their clothes.

Get himself in the shower then into the Jacuzzi.

Burn his clothes.

He glanced over at the sleeping she-devils and winced at the dirt and mud spread on his sheets.

Put new sheets on the bed and burn the dirty ones.

And his car. He allowed himself a whimper of distress when he remembered the mud and pond water and dirt and dust and...yeah, all that other assorted pleasant farm stuff that now covered the interior of his car.

Add getting the Beemer detailed to his list. Yeah, so it could get just as filthy in two days when they went back to the country. No way.

He fell back onto the bed with another groan. His poor Beemer couldn't handle much more. So fine, he thought, letting his eyes close for just a second. He wouldn't take the Beemer.

He added one more thing to his list: go buy a truck. A heavy-duty pick up that could handle the abuse.

There, his list was done.

And he would start on it right away--as soon as he let his eyes rest for a minute.

Just one...minute.

#

"Hey Kayli, come here!"

Kayli topped off her glass of iced tea and put the pitcher back in the refrigerator, then tossed some chips onto the plate next to her sandwich. "What is it? I'm trying to eat."

"Just come here. You've got to see this."

Kayli muttered her opinions about big brothers under her breath then walked through the house to the front door. She opened the screen door and poked her head out, eyeing Jake with all the impatience she could muster. "What?"

He pointed across the lawn, a big grin on his face, and she turned to see what had him smiling so broadly. A huge, brand new pick up was making its way up the drive, the rumble of its smooth diesel engine drowning out the birdsong. Kayli leaned against the door frame, holding the screen open with her foot as she glared at Jake.

"You called me out here to see one of your buddies in their new truck?"

"It's not one of my buddies."

"Then who is it?"

"Look."

Kayli stepped out onto the porch and watched as the truck pulled to a stop in the shade of the trees. The passenger door flew open and two girls jumped out, screaming their hellos as they bounded across the yard and into the field, heading for the show barn.

It was the twins. Which meant...

Sure enough, the driver door swung open and Ian climbed down. Her eyes widened when she saw he was wearing a pair of faded jeans that hugged his lean hips and muscular thighs. The gray t-shirt was so worn out she could barely read the "Property of Baltimore Banners" printed on the front. The loose fitting shirt should have hidden his build; instead, it only worked to accent his broad chest and well-muscled biceps and forearms. Kayli tried to get her tongue to stop sticking to the roof of her mouth long enough to swallow, but her mouth was so dry she couldn't.

"Nice truck. Did you just get it?" Jake asked, instantly bonding over a set of four rugged tires and a Cummins.

Ian climbed the steps to the porch and nodded, a smile much like Jake's on his own square face. "Yeah, I picked it up yesterday. I felt bad for abusing the Beemer, but I'm already in love."

Kayli rolled her eyes but still didn't say anything, which was probably good because the two men were still talking about the truck. There was a small lull in the conversation and she finally unglued her tongue long enough to speak.

"You traded in your BMW for a pick-up?" The disbelief in her voice matched the disbelief in Ian's eyes as he turned his dark gaze toward her.

"What? No, of course not."

Of course not, he said. Like it was unheard of to only have one vehicle; like everyone could afford two brand new ones. "So you now have two vehicles?"

"Well, no. Four, unless you count the motorcycle..." His voice drifted off and he shifted uncomfortably, as if he suddenly realized how that sounded.

Kayli just stared at him, not even trying to hide her disbelief as an unwelcome and uncharacteristic spurt of jealousy surged through her. Well wasn't he the lucky one. He had four vehicles, including a brand new, shiny, heavy duty, full size extended cab pick-up. He had probably been laughing at her the entire time he had been forced to drive in their old beat up one that barely ran enough to get back and forth for hauling. She turned and fixed Jake with a cool stare.

"Remember when I was talking about leagues? This is what I meant." She walked into the house, nearly tearing the screen door off its hinges before it slammed shut with a loud bang. Which was so stupid because if the damn thing broke, there'd be just one more thing they'd have to fix.

She stormed into the kitchen and grabbed the plate with the sandwich and chips along with the sweaty glass of iced tea, planning on heading out to the back porch to eat before getting to work. Jake's expected appearance in the kitchen stopped her before she could escape.

"Do you want to tell me what that was all about?" His voice was quiet and controlled as he leaned in the doorway, his hazel eyes watching her coolly. She put the plate back on the counter and drained the tea before looking at him.

"Nothing. It was about nothing."

"Really?" Jake crossed his arms and stared at her long enough that she looked away, embarrassed and angry at the same time. "What's gotten into you, Kayli?"

"Nothing has gotten into me, okay? I just...I don't like feeling like people are laughing at me, that's all."

"Whoa, back up. What? Who said anything about anyone laughing at you?"

Kayli took a deep breath and blew it out between clenched teeth, knowing she was overreacting and not even knowing why. "Nothing. Nobody. It's just...he shows up here with his fancy clothes and flashy cars and he's probably laughing the entire time. And just...never mind." And she just needed to shut up because she should not be yelling like she was.

"What the hell are you talking about, Kayli? Who's laughing? Because I haven't seen it."

"Just...leave me alone, Jake, okay? I don't want to talk about it." She tried to push past him but he grabbed her arm and stopped her. The look in his eyes was all disappointment, which only angered her more.

"No, I'm not going to leave you alone. What has gotten into you?"

"Nothing. I'm just...tired. And I hate being reminded of how little we have, when I work so damn hard."

"Kayli--"

"No! Don't say anything. You're not here, you don't know how hard it is to keep everything going with you gone. You don't know what it's like, fighting off the damn sharks who're always showing up, trying to buy this place so they can turn it into a housing development. You don't know what it's like, wondering if I'm going to have use the property for collateral again, wondering if the next time will be the time the bank says no. That falls to me! And I'm tired of being the only one who has to deal with it every single day!" She pulled her arm from his grasp and pushed past him, not caring that her unfair words hurt him more than they hurt her.

She stumbled into the hallway and came to a halt when she saw Ian standing there, watching her. Their eyes met for a brief second before she turned again and headed toward the back door, pushing through it as she wiped her hand across her eyes. Lori and the twins came running toward her but she ignored them, heading straight for the four-wheeler and escape.

Someone was calling her name--it sounded like Jake--but she ignored him as she jumped on the ATV and fired it to life, then roared across the back lawn toward the upper fields, wanting nothing more than to disappear for a little while.

FIVE

Kayli wiped her hands over her face one last time and took a deep breath, savoring the rich smells of hay and dirt and hard work. Her escape had lasted for close to an hour--much longer than she thought Jake would have given her. From the sound of footsteps coming into the barn, she figured he was done giving her time to feel sorry for herself, and was ready to give her a reality check. But first she needed to apologize, because she had been so out of line with the things she had said.

"Jake, I'm sorry. I didn't mean the things I said and--" She turned to face him just as the footsteps came to a stop, and jumped far enough back in surprise that she banged into the stall door.

"Um, sorry. Not Jake." Ian stood a few feet away and shrugged in apology, his eyes soft in the dim light of the barn. Kayli whirled around so her back was to him, her face heated in embarrassment and mortification, and prayed he wouldn't come closer.

Today was obviously not her day for answered prayers, because his footsteps echoed behind her and didn't stop until he was standing right next to her. He leaned his arms along the top of the stall door and stared down at the dirt floor, much like what she was doing.

But he didn't say anything. Minutes went by and he still didn't say anything. And the silence went on for so long that Kayli shifted from one foot to the other, uncomfortable and embarrassed. And mortified. If she could have disappeared into the dirt, she would have. She needed to apologize, she knew she did, but her voice was simply frozen.

"If I did anything--"

"You didn't." Kayli shook her head emphatically, interrupting him, silently berating herself for waiting so long to say anything that Ian had a chance to speak first. She took a deep breath and let it out in a rush, her eyes focused downward. "I...I'm sorry. About back there. I, uh, I was out of line. With all of it. So, I'm sorry."

She could have added more to the apology, could have offered at least a small explanation, but getting the apology out had been harder than she thought it would be. Kayli didn't think she could manage more than that right now.

Silence continued to stretch around them, and Kayli shifted again. She had thought--hoped--that Ian would just turn around and leave after she apologized, but he didn't move. She shifted her eyes to the right so she could look at him without his realizing it, and was surprised to see that he had turned to face her, his dark gaze studying her.

Kayli turned away, uncomfortable at the intensity she saw in his eyes. She moved away from him, walking toward the corner of the barn then turning around and heading toward the door before turning and heading back to the corner, looking for something to do.

"Do I make you nervous?"

Ian's quiet question stopped her aimless wandering and she looked over at him. He was still leaning against the stall door, one hand casually resting along the top, the other hand tucked carelessly in the front pocket of his jeans.

"Nervous? No, of course not." Which was so patently untrue. She was going to hell for lying, she knew it.

Ian pushed away from the stall door and for a second, she thought he was going to walk toward her. But he merely changed positions so his back was against the door, both hands now tucked into the pockets of his jeans. The stance was casual, unthreatening, laid back. He didn't move, just stood there quietly, his eyes following her as she walked toward the other corner. Like he was waiting...for something.

Nervous, he had asked her. Yes, he made her nervous, for reasons she didn't understand, and reasons she didn't want to admit. Not to herself, especially not to him. He made her nervous because of his good looks, his smile, his easy-going manner. He made her nervous because she adored how he was nothing more than a big teddy bear, a complete push-over when it came to his nieces.

He made her nervous because it would be too easy to like him--

no, too easy to like him *more*. He made her nervous because she didn't know how to act around him, didn't know how to talk to him or what to say because she was so afraid whatever she said would make her sound like some kind of simple country bumpkin.

He made her nervous because he made her want things, feel things, think things.

He made her nervous because all of those things were so completely unlike her that she didn't know how to react.

Yes, he made her nervous. Especially as he stood there, so still, his eyes watching her, seeing everything. She wondered what it was he saw when he looked at her, then decided she was probably better off not knowing. Especially now, after her stupid outburst, after throwing a temper tantrum and tearing off up here to the old barn and wallowing in self-pity for an hour.

She didn't have to see herself to know what she looked like: disheveled hair falling out of her daily pony tail, face flushed and probably--no, definitely--streaked, clothes covered in dust and grime. Yeah, there wasn't much to look at right now, yet he continued to watch her, his steady gaze intense and disconcerting.

Nervous? No, that was putting it too mildly. He made her want to turn and run away.

Worse than running away, he made her...want.

And she suddenly wondered why he was even here.

"Um, was there something you wanted?" Her voice was too loud in the quiet of the barn, disturbing several of the barn swallows that permanently roosted in the rafters above them. Ian cleared his throat and finally cast his gaze downward, away from her, as he shifted slightly.

"I just came to see if you were alr--if you needed anything."

"Oh. I thought Jake would have done that."

Ian looked up and met her gaze, a small half-smile on his face. And wouldn't it figure that he had the slightest dimple in his left cheek. Funny that she had never noticed it before. "He was going to, but I asked if I could come instead."

Kayli pulled her gaze away from the newly-discovered dimple. "Oh. I, uh, didn't hear your truck pull up."

"That's because I walked."

"You walked?"

"Yeah. Good thing I wasn't wearing those fancy Italian loafers, huh?" He pointed to his feet and Kayli automatically looked down, noticing the well-worn work boots covered in dirt.

Her face heated in embarrassment at the reminder of her scathing remarks and she looked back up at him, ready to apologize again. She was surprised at the seriousness in his gaze, even more surprised when he pushed away from the stall door and took a few uncertain steps in her direction. He stopped a foot away, and he looked almost as uncomfortable as she felt.

"I wasn't trying to flaunt anything, and I certainly wasn't laughing at you. At all."

"No, I know. I'm sorry. I shouldn't have said what I did. I...too much time out in the sun, or something. I guess. I was out of line and shouldn't--"

"I was trying to impress you."

His words hung in the air between them, effectively silencing her. Kayli snapped her mouth closed and stared at him as his eyes quietly searched hers. Her face heated again and she looked away, her gaze darting everywhere as she tried to figure out what he meant. He laughed, a short bark of sound that sounded anything but humorous. She looked back at him, saw him run one hand through his thick dark hair then shake his head.

"Yeah, that seriously backfired."

"Oh." Kayli looked away again, not knowing what to say. She wanted to ask him why he thought he had to try to impress her, but couldn't bring herself to voice the words. And the more time that passed, the harder it was to think of anything else to say. One minute went by, then another, and the air between them became heavy and oppressive.

Kayli shifted, and her movement seemed to unfreeze Ian, because he moved, too. He took a step toward her, then another, stopping so close that she could feel the heat of his body. She swallowed nervously and looked away, telling herself that she was imagining things, that she was reading way more into his nearness and that if she was smart, she would take a step back and tell Ian that she had work to do, that she had to get back.

But she didn't. And then he said her name, his voice barely above a whisper, and this time when she looked up at him, she knew she wasn't imagining anything. His eyes held hers, serious, searching. And then she did try to step back but she was too late because he reached out and gently cupped his left hand around her arm and pulled her toward him, his right arm closing around her waist and holding her against him. She placed her hands against his chest, thinking that if she was smart, she would push him away.

And then his head dipped closer, his lips barely touching hers in the lightest of kisses, and she stopped thinking. She tilted her head up and leaned into him, and he deepened the kiss, his mouth coaxing hers to open, his tongue sweeping in and meeting hers, hesitant at first, then more boldly as she responded to his seeking.

Kayli felt a whimper in the back of her throat, heard the breathy sound between them, and she pressed herself even closer. One hand curled into the soft material of his shirt, and she ran the other up his chest and around the back of his neck.

Ian deepened the kiss even more, as if he could breathe all of her in. His arm tightened around her waist and he shifted his hips against hers, letting her know exactly what kind of effect she had on him. She moaned again, a soft sound against his mouth, and pressed herself even closer. Her need spiraled and grew with each sweep of his tongue, with each stroke and caress of his hand along her back, with each press of his hips against hers.

But then, without warning, he gentled the kiss, easing himself away from her, pulling back just the slightest bit. Ian finally broke the kiss, stepping back just enough to let the cool barn air sweep between them, but he didn't release his hold on her, even when she uncurled her hand from his shirt and tried to pull away.

She felt the demanding pull of his gaze and finally looked up at him, torn between running away in embarrassment and tackling him to the dirt floor. Something of her indecision must have shown in her face because he offered her the slightest of smiles and pressed his lips against hers once more for an all-too-short and gentle kiss.

He cleared his throat and took a small step back, and the air that replaced his hold chilled her skin. Ian's strong gaze held hers and she had no idea what to say, or even what to do.

"I'm, uh..." Ian cleared his throat again and smiled. "I'm pretty sure your brother has every intention of kicking my ass if we don't get back soon."

"Oh." The word came out breathy and hoarse, and Kayli cleared her own throat, looking down at her feet. "Yeah. We can--"

Ian reached out and pulled her against him, his mouth crushing against hers, claiming, demanding. Kayli melted against him, hungry for his touch, desperate to feel his body pressed to hers. His hands cupped her bottom and pulled her to him, holding her against his hard length. She ran her hands along his back, finding the hem of his shirt and pulling it up, the hard muscle and hot flesh of his back alive under her touch.

Ian pulled his mouth away from hers and dragged his lips along her jaw. She tilted her head back, giving him access to her throat, and shivered at the heat of his mouth and tongue against her skin. Her touch lost all shyness; she wanted to feel him, all of him. She grabbed the hem of his shirt and pulled it the rest of the way up, dragging the material over his head. Ian pulled away from her long enough to untangle his arms from the shirt and toss it to the floor, then crushed her to him once more, his mouth hungry and demanding.

Kayli let her hands roam over his heated flesh, feeling the muscles in his back bunch under touch. She reveled in the feel of his firm skin beneath her hands, reveled in the hard definition of his arms and shoulders and chest. His breath hitched and he broke off the kiss, his head tilted back, his jaw clenched as she lightly ran her fingertips across his broad chest, teasing his nipples.

Her hands dropped lower, skimming the taut skin of his defined abs, following the dark line of hair that ran from his chest to disappear into the waistband of his low-slung, worn jeans. His hands closed around her wrists, stopping her even as she wondered how far she dared to go. She looked up at him, the heat she felt racing through her veins matching the heat in his dark gaze as he looked down at her. He loosened his hold on her wrists and pulled her arms behind him, then reached up and cupped her face in his hands, lightly rubbing his thumb against her lower lip.

They watched each other for a long minute. Kayli's heart pounded in her chest at the burning look in his eyes, and she felt herself leaning into him again, needing to feel his kiss, his touch. His mouth opened, but instead of leaning closer to kiss her, he leaned back to speak.

"I have been watching you for the last week, wondering what you would taste like, how you would feel. My imagination didn't even come close." The whispered words were husky and hoarse, and sent a spiral of heat shooting through her. And then he leaned forward, kissing her again, a hard possessive kiss that left her breathless before he pulled away and stepped back.

He cleared his throat and offered her another small smile. "But as much as I want you right now, I want to do this right even more. And that does not include a surprise visit from your brother." He leaned down and grabbed his shirt, shaking it out before pulling it on. Kayli laughed and pushed his hands out of the way, then promptly pulled the shirt off him again.

"I don't think Jake would show up," because she would seriously kick his ass if he did something like that, "but still..." She gave the shirt several hard shakes then turned it right-side out before handing it back to Ian. "It would probably look better if your shirt wasn't inside out when we got back."

Ian laughed, then leaned forward to give her a quick kiss, his arms wrapping around her and holding her loosely against him. "Jake said there was some kind of bull roast Saturday night at some firehouse."

"Yeah, at Maryland Line. It's an annual memorial fundraiser."

"I, um..." Ian looked away for a second and cleared his throat, then looked back at her, his gaze uncertain. "I was wondering if you would like to, um, if you would like to go with me. Be my date. If you want to, I mean."

Kayli almost laughed at his sudden nervousness, thinking he was teasing her. How could he be nervous after what just passed between them? But then she realized he was serious, that the nervousness wasn't an act, and her heart melted dangerously. She told herself that it was nothing, that she shouldn't read anything into it, but his uncertainty was her undoing.

But instead of jumping up and down, instead of throwing herself further into his arms and knocking him to the ground, she merely swallowed and nodded. "Yeah, that would be fun I think."

"You think?" Ian pulled away just the slightest bit and looked down at her, worry and indecision in his eyes. "If you don't--"

"No, I do." Kayli took a deep breath and leaned forward to give him a quick kiss. "I'd love to be your date."

She was rewarded with a dimpled smile and her heart jumped a little at the sight. His head dipped so his mouth could claim hers, and the kiss this time was gentle and sweet. He pulled away, and she tried not to moan at the loss of his arms as he stepped back, still smiling.

"Good." Ian nodded, then repeated himself. "Good.

Except...Jake said Lori was going and that the twins could come, that there would be other kids there. I should have said that first, so if you change your mind, that's okay."

"Well in that case..." She had meant to tease him, but his smile immediately wavered and she reached out to put her hand on his arm. "Ian, I was joking. I figured Sara and Shelly would be with you. That's completely okay. It'll be fun."

Again she was rewarded with another smile, and again her heart tripped at the sight. She ran her hand down his arm until she could entwine her fingers in his, then turned and tugged. He didn't say anything, just followed her across the barn and outside into the bright heat where she had left the four-wheeler.

Kayli dropped his hand and climbed on, kicking the engine to life before looking over to where he still stood. "Are you getting on?"

Ian smiled and said something, but she couldn't make out what it was over the roar of the engine before he straddled the seat behind her. She felt the warmth of his jean-clad legs pressed tightly against the outside of her thighs and the heat of his chest pressed against her back. His strong arms circled around her waist, and she had to stop herself from leaning back against him with a sigh.

She put the four-wheeler in gear, smiling as she tried to figure out the longest route back to the house.

SIX

Ian did not consider himself to be the jealous type. He had dated models in the past, beautiful women who drew the attention of every living male from the age of six to sixty, and had never been bothered by a single glimmer of jealousy. He had certainly never felt threatened before.

That had all changed tonight; Ian now knew that he was very capable of jealousy.

And that he was feeling it right now.

His hand tightened around the plastic cup of beer, forcing some to slosh over the rim. He sat it down on the table in front of him and reached for the pile of napkins, wiping his hands on one of them then balling it up and tossing it on the empty plate off to his side.

He turned in his chair and looked out at the dance floor. Kayli was laughing at something her dance partner was saying as they moved through the steps of some kind of line dance. His date was smiling and laughing with some other guy, and he was learning all about jealousy--first-hand.

"Why don't you just ask her to dance?"

Ian turned to face Jake. The man was sitting next to him, his long legs stretched out in front of him, a cup of beer held in his strong hands. A grin was on his face, and Ian didn't know if he should be amused or offended that Kayli's brother could read his thoughts so easily.

"I don't really dance to this kind of music." His frustration was clear in his grumbled words, and Jake laughed loud enough to draw the attention of the few other people sitting at the table: an elderly couple who looked like they were sleeping with their eyes open, and a lanky young teen who had been pouting ever since Lori took the she-devils to play some of the game wheels. Ian knew exactly how the kid felt.

"It's easy. Just follow what everybody else is doing. I mean, look: it's not like everyone is perfect and in-step. Just go do it."

Ian tossed Jake an incredulous look then turned to stare back out at the dance floor. Jake was right, of course. Nobody out there seemed to care if they were in-step or even moving in the same direction. They were just doing the best they could and having fun, not caring who watched.

Although he seemed to be the only one watching the dancers. Because more than a few curious stares were still focused on him. Not as bad as when they first walked in, but he was still drawing a few looks here and there.

Ian shouldn't have been bothered by them. Hell, he shouldn't have even noticed. It wasn't like hadn't gotten stares before. Usually, most of the players went unnoticed in crowds, but there were always a few people who would recognize them. And it was never a big deal: a few curious glances, an occasional double-take as recognition set in, one or a couple autograph requests. It was all harmless and generally unnoticed.

Tonight was different, though. Tonight wasn't about recognition--it was about being an outsider.

An outsider who had shown up holding Kayli's hand.

And because of that, he was now the subject of curious stares and blatant suspicion. Kayli had worked the room--he didn't know how else to describe what she did when they first got here-- introducing him to people she knew--which turned out to be almost everyone here. She always made sure she was either holding his hand or somehow touching him, making it obvious that they were together.

And it became very clear, very soon, that people were judging if he was good enough for Kayli...and most of the jury was still out on the decision. It left him with a feeling he had never experienced before, and one he didn't know how to describe.

He reached for the cup of beer and took a long swallow, still watching the dancers on the floor, still watching Kayli. Dressed in jeans, boots, and a modestly-cut short sleeve blouse, she blended in with most of the other women here.

Except she didn't, not really. There was a spark or light or something that made her stand out, that made everyone around her smile. It was one of the first things he had noticed the first time he saw her, and what had drawn him to her. He had no idea what it was, but he wasn't the only one who noticed.

And the fact that more than a few of those who noticed it were males--and that they were just as drawn to it--is what had him sitting here becoming entirely too acquainted with a little green monster.

Make that a big green monster.

The song ended, and Ian watched as Kayli's dance partner leaned closer to say something to her, his hand resting on her shoulder. Her head tilted to the side as she listened, and Ian watched as her smile faltered. She looked over at him, then shot a quick glance at her partner and shook her head as she stepped away. The guy looked over at Ian with a small smirk then turned back to Kayli and said something else.

Ian had no idea what was going on, and he didn't care. He took another swallow of beer, sat the cup on the table, then stood up and walked toward the dance floor. Something was finally going right for him tonight, because the band started a slow song just as he reached Kayli. She looked up at him with a smile in her eyes, her face flushed from dancing.

Ian pushed past the guy and pulled Kayli into his arms, claiming her lips in an all-too-brief kiss as the music played around them. He tightened one arm around her waist, fitting her snugly against him as he clasped her right hand in his and held it against his chest.

"Hi."

Kayli smiled at his simple greeting, dipping her head just a little closer. "Hi back."

"You having fun?"

"I am. But I don't think you are."

Ian briefly tightened his hold on her and leaned closer, his mouth close to her ear. "I am now."

Kayli looked up at him, her eyes soft in the dim lighting, and offered him another smile, this one shy. He held her gaze for several seconds, her body pressed against his as he led her in the slow dance. She rested her head against his shoulder, close to his chest, and he leaned down to kiss the top of her head. Her hair was down tonight, soft waves of honey that reached below her shoulder blades and teased his arm with their soft strands. She smelled of clean air with the softest hint of fresh cut flowers, and he had to stop himself from inhaling her scent too deeply so she wouldn't think he was sniffing her.

He could imagine her quick comeback if he did, and the thought brought a smile to his face. His hand tightened around hers and he closed his eyes, holding her against him, letting the music set the pace of their slow swaying on the floor.

Kayli's step faltered for just a brief second, and he opened his eyes to look down at her. Her head was tilted up, her eyes soft and warm as she just looked at him. She pressed herself even closer, and Ian lowered his mouth to hers, claiming her lips in a soft slow kiss that instantly tightened his body. There was no way she could miss his reaction, not pressed against him as she was. But she didn't pull away; instead she deepened the kiss, her fingers tightening around his as the music faded in the background.

Something banged into his thigh, effectively ending the kiss as he pulled away from Kayli and looked down. He tried to swallow his groan, and wasn't surprised to hear the small laugh from Kayli when the she-devils grabbed onto their legs, trying to join in the dance.

"Uncle Ian, are you gonna have a baby now?"

"Because we want a cousin to play with like Lori."

Their clear voices carried across the dance floor just as the music came to a stop, and Ian felt all the blood in his body rush to his face as embarrassment swamped him. His mouth opened and closed soundlessly, and he felt dozens of eyes on him, judging, as he tried to find his voice.

Kayli jumped to his rescue as she laughed and reached down to pick up Shelly, then took Sara by the hand and led the way to the edge of the dance floor.

"No, girls, your Uncle Ian is not going to have a baby. Why would you think that?"

"Because he was kissing you!"

"And that's how you make babies."

Ian stood frozen, completely speechless as the girls looked up at Kayli in earnestness. She laughed again then led them over to the table so everyone could have a seat. Except for Ian, who was still too stunned and mortified to do anything besides stand there in mute shock.

"Girls, you cannot make babies just by kissing. Now who told you such a thing?"

"That's what Maria said."

"She lives down the street from us."

"I'm sorry girls, but Maria was missing a few things when she told you that." Kayli leaned closer to the girls, offering them a gentle smile as she reached out to smooth their hair away from their faces. "Remember when your mom brought you up to the house to watch the cows? And we put them in the field with the bull?"

"What?" Ian's voice came out as a strangled croak, and everyone turned to look at him. Jake's shoulders were shaking with suppressed laughter, and Kayli just smiled and shrugged.

"Well, that's what we did." She turned back to the girls. "And you didn't see the cows kissing at all, did you?"

The she-devils giggled and shook their heads. Ian watched as Kayli opened her mouth to say something else, but he quickly stepped forward and tried to cover the twins' ears.

"Oh no. No, no, no. They don't need to hear this. *I* don't need to hear this." He stopped trying to cover their ears, since he was short two hands to do it effectively anyway. The girls continued to giggle at him, and he finally sat down in the metal chair next to Kayli. He reached around her and grabbed his beer, draining the plastic cup in one long swallow. "Babies. Oh God. If your mother heard about this...No. No girls, nobody is having any babies."

He leaned across the table to grab the plastic bucket of beer and refill his cup, surprised to realize that his face was still hot from embarrassment. He told himself that the flush had nothing whatsoever to do with the vivid images that came to mind when he heard "babies" and "Kayli" in the same sentence.

"Here, try some of this. It looks like you need it." Ian looked up to see Jake holding out a small cup a quarter-filled with clear liquid. He took it and tossed it back, draining it in one shot.

And nearly fell out of the chair as instant heat exploded through him.

"Jake Alexander Evans! You are an ass. I cannot believe you just did that!" Kayli reached for one of the bottles of water sitting in the middle of the table, twisted the cap off, and handed it to Ian. He drank it, waiting for the cool liquid to douse the flames roaring in his gut.

"Wha--" He cleared his throat and drank some more water then tried again. "What was that stuff?"

"Jake, how could you?" Kayli was still yelling at her brother, who was still shaking with laughter. She turned to Ian and gave him an apologetic look, trying to hide her own smile. "Hooch."

"What?"

"Hooch. Homemade moonshine. And it's not even the flavored kind." She turned back to Jake. "I guess Dale didn't listen when I told him not to bring any over."

Jake shrugged, still grinning, and held up a small mason jar filled with clear liquid. "It's just a little bit. And it looked like Ian could use it."

Ian shook his head and took another swallow of water, still trying to douse the burning in his throat and gut. He didn't say anything, just turned and looked down at the she-devils, who were watching him with curious eyes. "Girls, do me a favor, and don't tell your mother about any of this."

They laughed and Ian knew it was the wrong thing to say, and that he had just guaranteed that Bonnie would hear every little detail plus some. He felt a reassuring hand squeeze his shoulder, and he looked over to see Kayli smiling at him.

"It'll be fine, don't worry." She lowered her hand and glanced over to the dance floor as the band started playing another song. It was crowding quickly as people filed out to dance, and Ian noticed the wistfulness in Kayli's eyes as her feet tapped the floor under her chair.

He took a deep breath and looked over at Jake, who was watching him carefully. He glanced down at the twins, who seemed content to be quiet and still...for once.

Kayli had called it hooch. Ian figured it must be the same as liquid courage. He reached over and grabbed Kayli's hand and tugged as he stood. "So, do you think you can show me how to dance to this?"

Ian was rewarded with a bright smile and sparkling eyes, and knew that he would gladly suffer any embarrassment as long as she looked at him like that.

SEVEN

Kayli bit the inside of her cheek, trying to stop the laughter she felt gurgling beneath her breastbone. Ian muttered another curse under his breath as he stumbled along behind her and nearly tripped over a small log, catching himself before falling down. He stopped a foot away from her, giving her a disbelieving look before she turned and continued walking.

"Seriously? I thought you said it wasn't far." Ian grumbled, his footsteps noisy in the darkness.

"It's not. Honest."

"I think you're trying to get me lost. Because if you decided to leave me right now, there is no way I could find my way back to the truck."

Kayli laughed again at his grumbling, then reached for his arm when he started to walk past her in the darkness. He stumbled to a stop, looking at her in confusion before she pointed in front of them. Although how he could have missed the sound of the running water was beyond her. Unless the shots he had been tossing back had a bigger effect on him than she thought.

"I'm not trying to get you lost, so don't worry. I just thought you might want to get away from all the stares and questions back at the bonfire." Kayli dropped her hand and stepped around him, walking a few more feet to the flat rock overhanging the river and spreading the sleeping bag down, then lowering herself to a sitting position. The only sound was the gurgling of the water passing in front of her, and Ian's noisy footsteps as he followed her.

It was a silent oasis compared to the noise of the small crowd at the bonfire.

Jake had left the bull roast before it ended, claiming to be tired. And he had offered to take all three girls home with him--after suggesting that Ian and the twins stay at the house tonight, instead of driving the almost ninety minutes back to the city. Jake had leveled a quiet look at Ian when he repeated the invitation, quietly assuring him that they had the extra rooms. As far as subtle went, Jake failed miserably. But some kind of silent agreement passed between them, and Ian had taken him up on the offer.

Ian now lowered himself next to her, hanging his feet off the edge of the rock and staring into the muted darkness around them. The half-moon cast everything in a barely-there ghostly light, cloaking them in privacy in the middle of the great outdoors.

"You weren't having fun at the bonfire?"

Kayli glanced over at Ian, then looked back down at the moving water and shrugged. About twenty or so people had decided to have a bonfire after the bull roast, and Kayli had been invited. She had thought they'd have fun, just hanging out with a few of her friends, and they had--until the stares and questions really started, almost to the point of rudeness.

"It was okay. I just thought you might want a break, maybe some peace and quiet."

"Hm."

She could feel his eyes on her, but didn't look at him, afraid of what she might see. Because if their positions had been reversed, she would have just gone home.

Alone.

"I'm sorry they were giving you such a hard time."

Ian gave her another careless shrug then lay back, gazing up at the stars. A few quiet minutes went by before he spoke, his voice still hushed. "I am either more...mellow...than I thought, or these stars are a lot brighter than normal."

"They're always bright up here. You probably don't notice it down in the city because of all the lights. And..." Her voice drifted off as the first part of his statement sunk in, and she looked down at him in surprise. "Are you drunk?"

He turned his head to the side and looked up at her, giving her his dimpled smile. "No. Just mellow. But I think I'll let you drive home anyway."

Kayli bit back her own smile and turned away. "You didn't have to drink those shots, you know. Nobody expected you to." No, nobody had expected him to, which was what Dale had been counting on.

"Eh. It was called saving face. It was a tough crowd."

"Ian--"

"Look at me. No, not away. Look at me." Kayli finally turned toward him, no longer able to hide her smile. "And *that's* why I did it. Just for your smile."

Kayli laughed and shook her head, then laid down next to him, turning on her side and propping herself on one elbow. "I've had Dale's shine before. I would have held out for at least a kiss."

"Oh yeah?" Ian's gaze held hers for the longest time, the heat in his eyes searing her. She was going to look away, but his hand shot out and wrapped around the back of her neck in a gentle grip. He pulled her down until his mouth closed over hers with an intensity that sent spirals of heat and need shooting through her.

Her mouth opened under his assault, and Kayli groaned when his tongue swept in, exploring, coaxing, promising. She leaned in closer to him, melting against him, feeling his hard body next to hers. His hand gentled its hold on her neck, caressing and massaging. His other hand roamed along her back and down, shifting her so she was stretched out on top of him, her legs cradled between his long ones.

Kayli ran her hand up his chest, her fingers fumbling with the buttons of his shirt, popping them open so she could run her hand along the flushed skin of his broad chest. Ian deepened the kiss further, his hand cradling her bottom and pressing her against his hard length. She groaned again and pulled away, moving so she was straddling him, her eyes watching him as she finished unbuttoning his shirt and spread it open. Her hands roamed along his flesh, teasing, learning. His chest heaved with a hitched breath as she ran her fingertips over his nipples and down along his sternum, tracing the thin line of hair down his abdomen where it disappeared into the waistband of his jeans.

She waited for him to grab her wrists like he had the other day, and she looked up at him, waiting. His gaze was intent, watching her, holding her in place. Then he pushed himself up to a sitting position, his hands on her hips, steadying her against him as his mouth claimed hers once more. Kayli's breath left her in a rush and she pressed her hips deep into his lap, rubbing against the hard length of his erection.

She ran her hands up his chest and across his shoulders, dragging his shirt down his arms. He released his hold on her hips and shrugged his arms from the shirt then tossed it somewhere beside them. His arms closed around her, holding her tightly, his mouth still possessing her, his tongue still ravaging her.

He pulled away with a harsh breath and looked up at her, his dark eyes shining in the night. One of his hands moved to the front of her shirt and quickly undid the buttons. Kayli spread the material apart and let it slide down her arms as Ian watched, his eyes burning her everywhere his gaze touched.

He continued to hold her tightly in place with one arm, his free hand reaching up to trace a line from her throat all the way down to her navel, then lower to where their bodies met before running back up her bare skin. His hand stopped at the front clasp of her bra; with a quick flick, he released it, baring her to his gaze.

His head dipped closer and his mouth closed over one nipple; a wave of pleasure washed over her at the feel of his swirling tongue, at the rasp of his beard against her bare flesh. Kayli grabbed his shoulders as her head dropped back, as she pushed herself further against him, his touch awakening senses that had been dormant for too long.

She whispered his name but thought the sound was lost in the night around them. Ian's arm tightened around her even more and she leaned back further, bracing her arms on either side of his legs behind her as he suckled her, first one nipple then the other. His hold around her eased as his hands moved to her hips and gently guided her down against him, his own hips pushing up. Kayli moaned at the sensation, wanting to feel more, needing to feel all of him.

Ian's hands drifted over her legs then back up, stopping at the waistband of her jeans, pausing. She shifted and pushed herself up, then met his gaze. Her hands closed over his and gently eased them away, and she smiled at the flash of disappointment she saw in his eyes. She reached for her belt and quickly undid it, then unsnapped the button of her jeans and eased the zipper down, her gaze locked with Ian's own hungry one the entire time.

He reached up and clasped her face between his hands, and pulled her down for a searing kiss. With a groan he pulled away, then ran his hands down along her sides and grabbed her hips. He shifted his legs then rolled, moving quickly so that she was now laying under him, the hard length of his body pressed against her.

His eyes captured hers as he skimmed his hand along her bare skin, dipping his fingers into the open waistband of her jeans, easing them lower. Kayli's breath hitched as her hips rose to meet his touch, silently encouraging. She bit back a groan and closed her eyes when he moved his hand away from where she wanted his touch, then held her breath when he tugged at her jeans and underwear. He eased the material down past her hips to her thighs, then to her knees, exposing her, his fingers trailing a path back up, burning her with his touch.

His hand circled the crease of her thigh, teasing, his thumb brushing against her clit and moving away, brushing against her again. Kayli swallowed a soft moan, her hips slowly rocking toward him, seeking. Then he stopped teasing, his hand closing around her as he slid one finger inside her, then back out. Up across her clit then in, teasing, deeper. Kayli moaned and her hips rose to meet him, searching, begging for more as he slipped a second finger inside her.

"You are so beautiful." Ian's voice was a husky whisper, the words hoarse. Kayli opened her eyes to look at him, and was surprised to see the look of raw passion focused on her. The intensity in Ian's gaze sent shivers of excitement and anticipation through her, and she wanted nothing more than to feel him, all of him, over her, against her.

Inside of her.

She reached out and ran her hand along his chest, lightly grazing his flesh with her nails, feeling a surge of power when his head dropped back and his jaw clenched. And yet his fingers still teased her, stroking, probing, caressing her.

She shifted and dragged her hand lower, reaching down to unsnap his jeans and caress him through the denim. She fumbled with his zipper, trying to pull it down, but couldn't manage one-handed, not with his fingers inside her, branding her, coaxing a response from her.

"Ian..." She called his name, a demand, a question, the pressure building inside her, tightening. His fingers continued their exquisite torture, pushing her to the edge, holding her there.

"Come for me, Kayli." The soft demand was a ragged whisper in her ear. Her back arched as she fell off the precipice, her body shattering into pinpoints of light, reflections of the stars above them. She called Ian's name, felt his mouth close over hers, swallowing her cries in a fierce kiss as her body shuddered under waves of pleasure. Her hands gripped his shoulders and roamed over his back, holding him against her, using him as an anchor during the brief storm of insanity.

His kiss gentled as the storm subsided but she still felt lost, wandering, needing. She pulled her mouth from Ian's and kissed his jaw, his throat, feeling the brush of his clipped beard against her skin. Her hands roamed lower across his back, skimming around to his flat stomach and dipping into his unsnapped jeans, searching.

Ian's low moan echoed in her ear and he reached down and helped her with the zipper, then eased his jeans lower on his hips. Kayli skimmed her palm along his hot flesh, into the waistband of his shorts, and closed her hand over his thick shaft, her thumb teasing the smooth tip of his cock as she stroked him.

Ian nuzzled her neck, his mouth teasing, nipping, finally closing over her ear. His breathing was harsh, his words ragged. "I want you, Kayli. Now."

Her hand tightened over him as her stomach curled in anticipation, and she nodded. "Yes." Her whispered word unleashed something in Ian, and he pushed her back, easing her all the way down on the sleeping bag as he sat up. He leaned over her and pushed at her jeans, sliding them down her legs...where they caught on her boots, refusing to be moved further.

His laughter was a mixture of frustration and humor, and Kayli smiled at his impatiently muttered words. She sat up and grabbed his arm, then gave him an open-mouth kiss.

"Let me." She toed one boot off then leaned forward and tugged on it, untangling it from her bunched jeans. She placed it to the side then kicked her leg free of the denim before reaching for the other boot.

Ian grabbed her and pulled her back, his mouth closing over hers, his tongue plunging deep in the recesses of her mouth. His hands tangled in the length of her hair and he tilted her head back then skimmed his mouth down her neck and across her shoulder blade. A shiver coursed through her and she moaned, his impatient excitement filling her with desire.

He pulled away long enough to push his own jeans off then kneel between her legs. He sheathed himself with a condom then leaned over her, his hands on either side of her head. His lips brushed against hers, a soft whisper of a touch.

"I don't want you to do anything you don't want to." His eyes were serious, his concern reflected in their dark depths as he watched her. Her heart squeezed even as she fought not to smile. Could he honestly think she didn't want to do this? Could he honestly think she didn't want him?

Kayli raised her hips and wrapped her legs around his waist, pulling him closer to her, feeling his hard length pushed against her wet heat. She lifted her head just a fraction of an inch and brushed her lips against his, then cupped her hand along his cheek. "I want you, Ian. Now. Deep inside me."

The night hung suspended between them for a fraction of a second as Ian stared down at her. Then he thrust inside her in one swift move, filling her, completing her. Her back arched and her hips met his, welcoming him. He pulled back, then thrust again, setting a pace that was exquisite torture, a pace that left her wondering how much more she could take, even as she moaned the loss of him each time he withdrew.

The rhythm set fire to the embers still smoldering from her first orgasm, and she grabbed blindly for him, searching for an anchor to hold her steady. Ian grabbed one of her hands and held it above her head as his other arm wrapped around her waist and lifted her closer to him.

His mouth ravished her breasts, her neck. His lips closed over her ear and he whispered to her, words that her heart thought they understood but that her mind failed to comprehend. Her hand tightened on his and her head fell back, her hips thrusting upward to meet his, faster, demanding. The muscles in her body tightened as sensation spiraled throughout her, as light and sound and time hung suspended. Ian thrust again and her back arched one last time before the world crashed around her, shattering in an explosion of heat and need and fragment.

And still Ian thrust, deeper, faster, pushing her further over the edge into an alternate reality where nothing existed except the two of them and millions of glittering stars. He said something, whispered words in her ear that made no sense except for the heat that shot through her with each thrust. She turned her head, her eyes capturing his for one brief second before his mouth closed over hers, swallowing her cries.

His hold on her tightened, his mouth more demanding as he thrust again, again, then one last time. He pulled his mouth from hers and raised his head back, a low groan pushed from between his clenched teeth as he thrust a final time, his own shudder racking his strong body as held himself above her.

Kayli met his final thrust, her body gripping his, wrapping around him, squeezing. She remembered to breathe, the warm night air filling her lungs as her body finally settled, the fragmented pieces coming back together, forming a solid existence.

Time began to move, a slow passing as she wrapped her arms around Ian and held him close. He lowered his head to rest against her chest, his hand softly stroking her side as his own ragged breathing evened out.

Kayli closed her eyes, a small smile on her face, content for the moment to just be. They would have to leave, have to break apart and get dressed and go home. But for now, still joined together, they were one.

And nothing existed except for them and the moon and stars that stood watch over them.

EIGHT

Something pushed against Ian's shoulder. He mumbled and shrugged it off, fighting against the drag of awakening. Something pushed him again. He rolled over and tossed his arm over his face as consciousness pulled at his tired body. Ian only wanted to drift back into the darkness, to rest and replay last night--

He shot to a sitting position and nearly fell off the sofa before catching himself. Laughter came from somewhere to his side and he turned his head, searching through eyes that were barely open. He blinked and dragged both hands over his face, then blinked again as life came into focus around him.

Jake was standing less than a foot away, a steaming mug held out toward him, something that couldn't quite be called a smile on his face. Ian swallowed his groan and swung his legs to the floor, then leaned forward to accept the mug. He didn't have to look around to know that Kayli was nowhere in sight, but he couldn't stop himself from casting a quick glance around the room. She had fallen asleep, curled next to him in his arms, right here on the sofa.

Ian looked at his watch and frowned. Less than four hours ago? That couldn't be right. Or maybe it was, if the fog of sleep that still clung to him was any indication. He took a sip of the steaming coffee and winced as the hot bitter brew slid down his throat.

"I've never managed to make decent coffee. If you wanted the good stuff, you needed to get up earlier to drink the pot Kayli made."

"Earlier? What the hell time is it anyway?" Ian's voice was hoarse and rusty with sleep, and he forced himself to take another swallow of the brew.

"About seven, give or take."

"In the morning?" No wonder Ian was having trouble waking up. They hadn't gotten back here until after two, and hadn't fallen asleep until much later than that. And as much as Ian may have wanted otherwise, that time had been spent curled up here on the sofa, innocently talking.

"Yes, in the morning. Why don't you come on outside with me."

Mostly innocently, Ian amended to himself. From the tone of Jake's voice, and the expression on his face, Ian didn't think he was being invited outside to enjoy the morning air. With a groan that had as much to do with his stiff body and sleep-fogged brain as it did with the prospect of going outside with Jake, Ian pushed himself from the sofa, wincing as he stretched. He followed Jake through the living room and out onto the front porch, taking another sip of the strong bitter coffee for fortification purposes.

Jake walked across the porch then settled himself on the railing, one leg dangling as he gulped from his own cup. He fixed Ian with his steady gaze, his eyes eerily vacant, then motioned toward the porch swing. Ian paused, then moved toward the railing, choosing to lean against it as the two faced each other. Jake raised one brow at him, questioning, but said nothing, just took another sip of the coffee and turned to stare out at the front yard.

"Did you enjoy yourself last night?" The question may have been phrased casually, but Ian's guard went up, knowing that there were many different questions hidden within it.

"Yeah, I did. The bull roast was fun. Different. Thank you again for inviting us to stay the night, and for bringing the twins home."

Jake turned to face Ian, his face still carefully blank. Ian met his steady gaze, letting the other man know that he wasn't going to be easily intimidated...or scared off. A brief smile lifted one corner of Jake's mouth before he turned away again, resting his head against the post. He closed his eyes and fell silent for so long that Ian briefly wondered if the man had fallen asleep. When he finally broke the silence, his voice was quiet, tinged with worry and strain.

"I'm not going to ask what's going on with you and Kayli. She's a grown woman and more than capable of making her own decisions. Lord knows she keeps this place going pretty much on her own." Jake opened his eyes again and stared off to the side. Ian had the strongest suspicion that he was seeing things that weren't there, that while his gaze was focused on the property sprawled around them, he was seeing something completely different.

Jake let out a deep breath and finished his coffee, then shifted so he was now facing Ian. "I don't want Kayli hurt or used."

Ian stiffened, insulted and angered at the insinuation. "I'm not--"

"I didn't say you were. But I'm pretty sure that Kayli's not like most women you date. If she's some kind of novel distraction..." Jake let his words hang in the air between them, his gaze still steady and unflinching.

Ian stiffened again, but he didn't know what to say. Jake was right: Kayli *was* different from the women he usually dated. He couldn't help but think that was a good thing. She was honest, genuine, real.

But to call her a novel distraction? No, she was more than that. "If you're asking if I like your sister, yes, I do. A lot. If you're asking about short term versus long term...I can't answer that. I don't know. We're just getting to know each other. For all I know, she could come out here in a few minutes and tell me to get lost. I have no idea what's going to happen today or next week or--"

"My leave is up in ten days. I'm being deployed again after I get back to California." Jake's voice was quiet, almost haunted, and made something roll in the pit of Ian's stomach. He looked down at the cup in his hand, not knowing what to say.

He had vaguely realized that Jake served in the military and was home on leave, but he didn't understand the reality of it. The subject had never come up, and Ian had never bothered to ask. And now he didn't even know how to act.

He cleared his throat and looked up at Jake. "Deployed. As in...?"

Jake offered him a short grin. "As they say in the movies: I could tell you, but then I'd have to kill you."

And Ian realized he was serious. This time he was the one who looked out over the yard, not really seeing it. "Does Kayli know?"

"I haven't told her or Lori yet. I don't want them worrying. I'd appreciate it if you kept it quiet."

"Uh, yeah, sure, no problem. But...why tell me?"

"The last few times I deployed were tough for both of them, but especially for Kayli. She's the sole caregiver for Lori, plus she takes care of this place. It's easier for her when I'm state-side, even though I'm all the way out in Cali. When I'm not...it's an adjustment." He shrugged, as if this was something people dealt with every day. "I don't want Kayli being hurt even more on top of everything else she has to deal with."

"I don't plan on hurting her."

Jake eyed him with a flat level gaze that made Ian uncomfortable, that made him think the man standing across from him had seen things he couldn't begin to imagine.

And that he was capable of much worse.

The silence drew tight as the minutes dragged by. Finally, Jake nodded, almost to himself, then offered Ian another small smile. "Good. I think Kayli left some food in the kitchen for you. Go grab something to eat then meet me up by the big barn."

"Excuse me?"

"I figure if you're going to be hanging around, I might as well get some work out of you." Jake walked by him, clasping him on the shoulder as he passed, then made his way down the porch steps. He paused then turned back to face Ian, a smile still on his face. "By the way, I didn't say anything to Kayli about the beard burn on her neck and chest this morning. Just like I'm not going to say anything to you about your shirt being buttoned crooked. I just wanted you to know that."

Ian stared after Jake's retreating figure, then glanced down at his shirt. Sure enough, the buttons that were actually fastened were off-center and mismatched. He sat his cup on the railing and quickly redid the buttons of his shirt, wondering what the hell had just happened.

And what the hell he had just gotten himself into.

NINE

Kayli braked the four wheeler to a stop and cut the engine, then leaned back on the seat and just stared. A little tingle shot through her as she watched Ian leaning over by the fence, the worn denim of his jeans stretched across his backside, the sun glinting off his bare back. The man was built, no doubt about it. All lean sculpted muscle that moved with a special beauty that only men could pull off. She wanted to run her fingers across all that bare skin, knowing that it would be warm from the sun. Another thrill raced through her when she imagined how his body would react to each of her touches. No, not imagined. Remembered.

Which was absolutely crazy, considering the bull roast had only been four nights ago. But so much had happened so fast in the days since. Ian was spending so much time here that Jake had suggested that he and the twins might as well move in until his sister came back from vacation. Kayli had held her breath waiting for his answer, then tried to hide her disappointment when he said no.

This morning he had shown up with a duffel bag for the twins and one for himself, and grumbled to Jake that he was tired of getting up so early to drive out here. Bonnie was due back in a week. Ian said maybe it wouldn't be so bad to just stay here after all.

Kayli didn't miss the heated look he slid her way, and she was pretty sure Jake hadn't missed it either. In fact, she doubted if Jake had missed anything in the last few days. If anything, he had gone out of his way to let her know where he was going to be and for how long. And he usually had all three girls with him.

He was surprising her, but she didn't want to question him. She knew her brother all too well and knew that he was up to something. And she still didn't want to question him.

Ian straightened and stretched, then turned and looked over at her, treating her to a view of his broad chest and sculpted abs. And strong, capable arms. He smiled then leaned against the fence, and Kayli was surprised at how comfortable he looked there. Almost like he fit in, like he belonged.

She pushed that dangerous thought away as she smiled back at him. "What are you doing?"

Ian straightened then walked toward her, a glint in his eyes. "I am fixing fence boards. Or making a bigger mess of them, I haven't figured out which, yet. I'm sure your brother will let me know."

"They're fence boards. All you do is nail them back in place--"

Ian grabbed her and closed his mouth over hers, kissing her deeply. She leaned into him, turning so she could press herself against his bare chest. He dragged his mouth from hers and down her neck, nuzzling her ear.

"Do not say 'nail' in front of me while you're straddling this thing. I never knew a four wheeler could be a turn-on."

Kayli barely managed a laugh as he continued kissing her neck, and she leaned further back, giving him access as she ran her hands across his chest and stomach then reached for the waistband of his jeans and tugged. "Have a seat with me."

"Hm?"

Kayli pulled away and smiled at his groan, then slid to the rear of the seat and patted in front of her. "I said, have a seat. It's big enough."

Ian's dark eyes twinkled. He lifted himself up and over the four wheeler, straddling the seat backwards so they were facing each other. Kayli lifted her legs over his and moved forward, sliding her hands across his chest and around his waist. His arms closed around her and pulled her even closer, so that she was nearly straddling him. Nearly.

He claimed her mouth in another kiss, his tongue sweeping inside, teasing, before he pulled away. "There's a fantasy here somewhere, I'm sure of it."

Kayli laughed and rested her head against his chest, just enjoying being close to him, enjoying the feel of his arms around her. The steady beat of his heart echoed in her ear and the sun warmed them from above. She could sit like this for hours, content to just be with him. But they didn't have hours.

"I want to make love to you Kayli." His hoarse voice was a whisper in her ear, and her body instantly responded, tightening in anticipation. She raised her head and looked up at him, liquid heat filling her at the hot desire so clear in his eyes. They didn't have hours, but that didn't mean they couldn't make the most of the time they did have.

They were getting pretty good at that.

Ian must have seen her thoughts in her eyes because he gave a low growl and crushed her to him, his touch powerful, his kiss possessive and demanding. But he pulled back too soon, his hand cupping her cheek as he ran his thumb across her lower lip.

"This, too. But I want to make love to you. In a bed. I want to fall asleep holding you in my arms and wake up next to you."

"Ian, we can't--"

"I know. I didn't mean here." He kissed her again, gently this time. "Let's go out Friday night. Just you and me."

Kayli bit her lip, indecision warring within her. She wanted nothing more than to say yes. And God, for once she wished she could just forget about everything, and not have to worry about getting up early, about all the responsibilities that fell on her shoulders, about everything that had to be done.

But she couldn't.

"What about the girls? Plus everything around here. I can't--"

Ian silenced her with another kiss. "Jake said he'd babysit, and that he'd make sure you wouldn't have to worry about anything. So how about it? Just you and me." He kissed her again, his arms tight around her. "I want to wine and dine you." Another kiss. "I want to impress you and romance you." Another kiss before his mouth moved to her ear, and his voice dropped to a husky whisper.

"I want to make love to you all night, with wine and candlelight and roses and soft music. I want to sleep with you in my arms then wake up and make love to you some more." His mouth moved back to hers, claiming her with a softness that made her melt against him. "Come with me, Kayli. Spend the night with me at my place. Just the two of us. Please."

She wrapped her arms around his neck and gazed into his eyes, her heart beating so fast she was surprised he couldn't hear it. Or maybe he could, because he leaned his forehead against hers and placed his hand between them, where their beating hearts met. She tried to smile, but was afraid it came out too wobbly. "You kinda had me as soon as you said Jake would babysit."

Ian laughed, but it came out sounding more relieved than humorous. He flashed her a brief smile, then cupped her face in both of his hands and lowered his mouth to hers. This kiss was different than the previous ones, coaxing a sweet surrender from her. Kayli tightened her arms around him and pressed herself closer, gladly giving in to him.

Yet the kiss became more demanding even as she surrendered to him. Ian's hands roamed across her back and down, cupping her bottom and pulling her more fully on top of him. Kayli tightened her legs around his waist and rocked against him, her body searching him out.

Ian's hands moved around to her own waist and grabbed the hem of her shirt in his fists. He slid the material upward, skimming her skin with his knuckles and sending shivers racing along her arms. His thumbs slid under the band of her sports bra, teasing the underside of her breasts, when a shout broke them apart.

Kayli let out her breath on a groan that echoed Ian's own. She reached up and pulled her shirt down then scooted back, putting some distance between them. Ian grabbed her for a quick kiss then slid off the four wheeler, adjusting himself with another groan.

"Friday night. I can survive until Friday night."

Kayli laughed and shifted sideways on the seat, looking over her shoulder when she heard her name being called again. Lori had just crested over the hill and was running toward them, her hair flying out behind her.

Kayli straightened then frowned as Lori called her name again, gaining speed as she got closer. She had never seen her niece run so fast, and she instantly went on alert. Ian must have sensed the change in her, because he stepped closer and rested his hand on her leg.

"Aunt Kayli!" Lori's voice was clearer as she closed the distance between them, finally skidding to a stop several feet away. She leaned over and took in several gulps of air, then looked back up. Her face was flushed and streaked with sweat and tears.

Kayli jumped off the four wheeler and rushed over to Lori,

wrapping her arms around her. "What is it, Lori? What happened?"

"Where are the twins?" Ian was standing behind her now, and Kayli noticed the worry etched in his face. She hadn't even considered the younger girls, and now she turned back to Lori, even more anxious.

But Lori shook her head and pointed behind her. "They're...okay." Kayli looked up and, sure enough, the twins were skipping down the hill, Ronan running back and forth between them. "It's Dad."

"What? What happened? Is he okay?"

Lori took another deep breath and wiped her hand over her face, then shook her head. "Uncle Cole's up at the house. Aunt Kayli, I think Dad's going to kill him!"

A shaft of ice pierced her heart at the mention of Cole's name. She pulled away from Lori and turned back to the four wheeler, quickly climbing on and starting it in one motion. She looked over at Ian, trying to keep her face blank, trying to keep her emotions in check.

Not an easy thing to do when she was torn between anxiety, fear, hurt, and anger.

"Stay here with the girls."

"Kayli--"

"Please Ian. Just...stay here." She didn't wait to see if he agreed, just put the four wheeler into gear and took off toward the house, hoping he would listen.

But she quickly shoved her worry about Ian listening to the back of her mind. Cole was here, and she doubted if Lori had been exaggerating about Jake killing him.

The only question was if she'd stop Jake...or if she'd help him instead.

#

Ian had no idea what to expect when he got back to the house-- something between a quiet family reunion and bloody bedlam. Although, for as hysterical and upset as Lori had been, he didn't think murder was really at the top of the list. Lori was a young teenage girl, and he was certain she was overreacting to what was nothing more than an uncomfortable family situation.

So he had stayed with her, trying to calm her down and reassure her. Having the she-devils with her helped, since both girls adored Lori and went out of their way to make the girl smile. It wasn't long before he figured the situation was as good as it was going to get.

So he made up some chore for them to do over at the big barn with stern instructions to stay there and stay out of trouble. Then he made his way back to the house, cursing the long hike under his breath, certain that whatever was going on was exaggerated, certain that whatever the situation was, it would be over when he finally made it back.

He had a mental image of the three siblings sitting on the front porch, talking amongst themselves, straightening things out. Yeah, from the little Jake had told him, he knew the relationship was strained. But he knew what it was like to have a sibling, and while it might be a little different because it was just Bonnie and him, surely things couldn't be as bad as Lori had made them seem.

Which was all the more reason why he was surprised to hear so much yelling when he neared the house, and even more surprised when he turned the corner and saw the scene in the front yard.

Jake was standing five feet away from another guy, and Ian could see the tension rolling off him in waves even from where he was standing. Kayli had her arms wrapped around him from the front, simultaneously leaning into him and trying desperately to push him back. Jake had one arm wrapped around her, and Ian could tell he was doing his best to get Kayli behind him even as he motioned toward the other man, warning him to leave.

But what surprised Ian the most was the appearance of the other man. If he hadn't known this was their brother, he would have sworn that their rural home had been infiltrated by a gang member.

He had Jake's height, but his build was slender, almost too thin in the baggy pants belted at his hips and the worn and stained cotton t-shirt. His ropey arms were covered in tattoos that stretched from his wrist to his neck. His hair was close-cropped, shaved almost to the point of baldness.

A mocking smile split the man's face in two. He lunged forward, then stopped and stepped back, laughing when Jake tried to move toward him. "Yeah? What are you going do, Jake? You gonna come after me? Big bad ass Marine? C'mon, do it."

"Cole, stop it! Just leave!" Kayli cried, looking over her shoulder at him as she continued holding onto Jake.

"Leave? Why would I do that? This is my home, too."

"Stop baiting him, Cole!"

"No. Not anymore it's not." Jake's voice drowned out his sister's in a threatening growl that would have sent sane men running, but Cole didn't move. Instead, he took another step forward and laughed.

"Yeah, it is."

"No. You have no right to anything around here. You gave up that right when you left the way you did. So do everyone a favor, and just leave."

Ian watched as Kayli stiffened, then pushed away from Jake's hold. Her fiery gaze moved between her two brothers and her chest heaved with each breath. She reached up with a shaking hand and pushed a thick strand of hair out of her face, then placed her palm flat against Jake's chest. "Jake, stop it. Cole's clean. He's been clean for almost two years."

"What?"

"You heard her. Guess the joke's on you, isn't it?"

Ian felt the tension escalate, actually felt it snap as Jake lunged for his brother, throwing a punch that landed on the other man's face with such force that he fell to the ground.

Cole jumped up quickly and lunged for Jake, hitting him square in the stomach with his head. Both men hit the ground, rolling and punching. Kayli began yelling, reaching out for a flailing arm. An image of her being caught between the two fighting men whirled through Ian's mind, unfreezing his feet.

He took off running toward Kayli and grabbed her around the waist, trying to pull her away from the fight. She struggled in Ian's hold, trying to get away before she realized who had her. She collapsed against him, her hands tight on his arms, her breathing heavy as she tried to turn and see what was going on. Ian moved so they were facing the two brothers, but kept his arms snug around her, protecting, comforting.

But only for a minute.

The fight continued, punches and profanities the only noise in the air around them. Kayli made a sound that resembled a low growl and pulled herself from Ian's arms before he could stop her. She closed the distance to the corner of the house, but before Ian could move to follow her, she returned. Fury creased her normally calm features and angry determination burned in her eyes as she approached her two brothers...

And turned the hose on both of them, blasting them with the full force of a stream of water. Kayli moved closer, training the water on both of them until they separated, muttering and cussing. Jake tried to stand but slipped in the rapidly-growing puddle of mud and fell against his brother, who was also sliding as he tried to gain his own footing.

Kayli's assault lasted for several long minutes, long after the two brothers had finally given up and laid back in the mud. Their harsh breathing mingled together, punctuated by coughing and sputtering until Kayli finally turned the water off. She stood still, staring at them, then threw the hose down. It landed with a wet splatter, splashing mud far enough that even Ian wasn't safe.

"I've had it with you two. Both of you. Grow the hell up and act like adults. And if you can't do that...I don't want to see either one of you!" Kayli stared down at them for another minute, the sheen of moisture in her eyes building until a single tear clung to her lower lash and finally fell, trailing a small track down her cheek. She brushed at it with a shaking hand then turned on her heel and stalked away, disappearing around the corner of the house before anyone could say anything. The four wheeler's engine roared to life a minute later, and Ian moved to go after her, to follow her.

"Let her go, Ian." Jake's harsh voice stopped him from following. Indecision and Jake's command rooted him to the ground, and he stood there, uncomfortable, feeling like an unwelcome intruder who had stumbled into the middle of a dark family secret. Ian finally pulled his gaze from where Kayli had disappeared and turned to look down at the two brothers who were still sprawled on the ground, covered in mud and blood.

Jake was the first to move, rolling over to push himself to his hands and knees. He shook his head and spit something from his mouth, then rose more slowly to his feet, stumbling. His lip was cut and his right eye was beginning to swell. He looked down at Cole, his eyes cold and detached as he studied his brother, who looked even worse.

Time stretched around them, the tension building so thick that Ian began to feel his own chest tighten with it. Jake suddenly moved toward his brother, so quickly that Ian expected him to lash out again, to pick up the fight from where they had left off. But he didn't.

Jake leaned over and slowly put out his hand, extending it to his brother. Ian held his breath as Cole sat back on the ground and eyed his brother warily. A tense minute went by before he reached up and grabbed Jake's hand, then another as the two brothers locked gazes in what Ian could only imagine as an edgy battle of wills.

Something passed between the two of them, but Ian could only guess what it was as Jake slowly, almost grudgingly, pulled Cole to his feet. And still neither said anything, making Ian feel even more like an outsider.

"Ian, could you go get a few beers and bring them out to the porch?" Jake may have phrased it as a question, but Ian had no doubt that it was a command. He paused, glancing between the two brothers and the spot where Kayli had disappeared from.

"But Kayli--"

"She needs some time by herself. How about those beers?"

"No. No beer. I'll just have tea or something." Cole finally broke the stare-down with his brother and fixed a piercing look at Ian. But only for a minute, because he turned back to face his brother, his gaze as hard and blank as Jake's. "Like Kayli said, I'm clean. Not even alcohol."

Jake watched his brother with those cold, distant eyes for a long minute, giving nothing away. Ian instinctively knew he was sizing up Cole, deciding if he believed him or not, deciding if he could trust him or not. Jake finally nodded, a curt motion of his head, then looked at Ian. "How about some water then."

Ian let his gaze move between the two brothers, not sure if he should trust either of them. He wanted nothing more than to go after Kayli, to see if she was okay and to offer whatever comfort or reassurance he could. But his own instincts happened to agree with Jake, and he knew Kayli needed at least some time alone. So he nodded then turned away and headed for the house, wasting no time in grabbing the water pitcher from the refrigerator and finding three plastic cups. He held the cups under one arm and practically raced back outside, half expecting to find Cole and Jake trying to murder each other again.

But they weren't. In the short time Ian had been gone, both men had obviously used the hose to rinse themselves off. Jake was standing off to the side, wringing water out of his ruined t-shirt before shaking it out and placing it over the porch railing. Cole had done the same and was now sitting on the bottom step of the porch, one hand gingerly holding his side.

Jake stepped around him and took the pitcher from Ian, then poured out one cup at a time. He handed the first one to Cole, who took it with a curt nod. "Those ribs will feel better if you wrap them."

Cole nodded again then raised his cup in a mock salute. "To dysfunctional families."

Jake said nothing, just watched his brother for another minute before lifting his own cup and draining it in one long swallow. Ian reached over and refilled it, then sat the pitcher to the side and leaned against the porch railing, not knowing what he should say or do, if anything.

"Remember how the three of us would sit out here after doing our homework? Just before dinner. Dad would have our hides if we didn't finish, or if we goofed off too much before we did. I was supposed to be in charge because I was the oldest, but it was always Kayli who made sure we got done when we were supposed to."

"Yeah." Cole wrapped both of his hands around his now-empty cup and stared down into it, and Ian knew from the expression on his face that he was seeing the past come to life. "Because there was nothing we wouldn't do for her."

Ian looked over at the porch swing, seeing the ghosts of three young children, hearing their laughter and bickering. He shook his head clear, unsettled at the image, unsettled at everything that had happened in the last half hour.

"You have a sister. Younger, right?" Ian looked up to see Jake studying him. He nodded, vaguely surprised at the question. "Then you probably know what I'm talking about. Baby sisters. A real pain in the ass."

"But there's nothing you wouldn't do for them. Nothing you wouldn't do to keep them safe and happy." Cole responded to Jake's statement, drawing a curious look from his brother. The two of them locked gazes, and Ian felt something shift between them. He wasn't sure what, couldn't even begin to guess at the history between them. But he knew something had just changed, especially when Jake let out a short, almost-forced bark of laughter.

"Kayli is still a pain in the ass."

"That she is," Cole agreed.

"Always thinks she knows best."

"Always bossing everyone around."

Ian shifted, uncomfortable once more as the brothers began listing Kayli's traits as a sister. He finally cleared his throat and interrupted them. "Um, guys, I really don't think--"

"Who in the hell are you, anyway?" Cole looked up at Ian, his gaze clear, so much like his sister's, focusing on him with suspicion. Ian shifted his weight to his back foot and looked between Cole and Jake. He opened his mouth to respond, then shut it again, not really sure how to answer.

"This is Ian. He's dating Kayli." Jake answered Cole's question for him, which earned him an even more suspicious glare from the younger brother.

"Is that so? Well then, why the hell are you standing here? Shouldn't you be checking on our little sister?"

TEN

Ian entered the cool dimness of the barn, a sense of déjà vu coming over him as he stopped just inside, letting his eyes adjust. He had done this exact same thing two weeks ago, but it seemed like so much more time than that had passed.

Hell, it felt like a lifetime had passed in just the last hour alone.

He let out a sigh and looked around, knowing he should feel at least a little comfort in the fact that things seemed to have worked out. Maybe. At least the two brothers didn't seem to be on the verge of killing each other. But he still couldn't shake the feeling that things were just simmering on the back burner, waiting for the right time to explode.

He hoped he was wrong, but he wasn't foolish enough to believe in fairy tales and happily-ever-afters. These things had a way of blowing up, sooner or later. He just hoped it was later. Much later.

He let out another deep breath then stepped deeper into the barn, his eyes searching the shadows around him, looking for Kayli. He knew she was in here--he had already learned that she liked to come up here to get away, to enjoy some privacy.

Or to escape.

A rustling sound came from the corner stall and Ian made his way over there. He stopped at the closed door, resting his arm along the top and peering down. Kayli was propped against the side wall, her long legs stretched out in front of her. She had thrown a blanket down over top of the straw and was just sitting there, her head lowered, twirling a piece of straw in her hands.

"You okay?"

His quiet question was greeted by a long silence before she shifted. She nodded, but didn't look up at him. "Yup, fine and dandy."

Ian almost laughed at her forced casualness. He could imagine exactly how she felt, but there was nothing funny about it. He watched as she shifted again, pulling her knees to her chest and wrapping her arms around them before resting her chin on her arms. Her shoulders raised and lowered with a deep sigh, yet she still didn't look at him.

"Lori's on the way down to the house with the twins to help them pack."

"Pack? For what? Are they going somewhere?"

Kayli shook her head and shrugged, the smallest lift of one shoulder. Ian's heart tugged at the forced nonchalance of the movement. "I figured you'd want to take them home, get them away from here. After...you know."

It was Ian's turn to sigh. She thought he was going to take the twins and leave because of her brother, because of what happened. He should have known she'd think that.

Ian pushed the stall door open and walked in, then lowered himself to the blanket next to her. Less than an inch separated them, and he was careful not to move any closer as he held out the bottle of water in his hand. "Here, I thought you might be thirsty."

Her fingers grazed his as she took the bottle with a murmured thanks, but she quickly broke the contact. He watched her from the corner of his eye as she twisted off the cap and drank, then put the cap back on and set the bottle to the side. Ian leaned his head back against the wall and closed his eyes, breathing in the mingled scents of straw and dirt...and Kayli. And he was surprised at the sense of peace, at the sense of belonging that suddenly filled him.

"The she-devils would raise hell if I tried to take them home. Besides, I'm kind of enjoying myself around here. So, if it's okay with you, I think the three of us are going to hang around until my sister gets home."

Kayli stiffened beside him, and he wanted to do nothing more than pull her into his arms and hold her. But he was afraid she'd push him away, afraid of how she'd react if he did. So he held his breath and waited.

"Ian, you don't...I mean, thanks but...you don't have stay. I wouldn't want to stay, not after..." Her voice drifted off in a small sob, and Ian sensed her turning away. To hell with worrying if she'd push him away.

He reached for her, wrapping her in his arms and pulling her closer, lowering her head to his chest. She stiffened at first, then finally wrapped her own arms around him in a tight grip that let him know exactly how upset she was. She buried her face in his shirt, her shoulders shaking as sobs racked her body.

Ian tightened his hold on her, gently stroking her hair as she cried against him. Long minutes went by, the silence broken only by her labored breathing and quiet sobs. Ian dropped a gentle kiss on her temple and rested his head against hers, absently rubbing her back.

"It's going to be okay, Kayli. Everything is going to work out, somehow."

"How can you say that, after what happened? After seeing those two..."

Ian's breath hitched at her choked words, and he knew how much it cost her to admit that. He eased her back the tiniest bit so he could look down at her. "If it's any consolation, I left the two of them on the porch, talking. Well, mostly staring at each other, but still talking. I don't think they're on the verge of killing each other anymore."

Kayli's arms tightened briefly around him then she pulled away and settled closer next to him, their shoulders touching. She leaned her head back against the stall wall and took a deep breath, her gaze focused somewhere he couldn't see.

"You know, Cole wasn't always...he's had a rough time. He was always a little rebellious, hanging with the wrong kinds of kids. Recreational drugs. Then things started missing from around here. It's like...he just stopped caring or something. Fights with Dad. And I don't mean arguments, either. They had a huge one the last time he saw our father, a physical one." Kayli looked down at the now-destroyed piece of straw that she had been twisting and tossed it aside with a sigh. "He pretty much disappeared after that, and I guess we disowned him. Jake especially. It tore him up, not being able to be here, knowing what Cole was doing..."

Ian draped his arm around Kayli's shoulder and pulled her

closer, dropping a kiss on the top of her head. "You don't have to tell me this, you know."

"Yeah, I know. But I want to." She dropped her head on his shoulder. "Anyway, like I said, Cole disappeared for a while. And then, about a year ago, he showed up. I almost didn't recognize him. And I didn't believe him at first about being clean, about changing. But he did, he really did. And now he stops by every few weeks. I hadn't told Jake because...well, you saw what happened."

"Yeah. But you know what...that's between those two. You need to let them figure things out on their own. And just remember--you've had a year to make things right. Jake's had, what? An hour? They're both grown men, they can figure it out. And if they don't, well...that's on them, not you."

Kayli looked up at him, her blue eyes moist with still unshed tears, her face damp and flushed. She blinked and looked away, then lowered her head back to his chest. "Thank you for saying that."

Her words were muffled in his shirt, and Ian actually smiled at how unnecessary they were. "Don't thank me for speaking the truth."

Several more minutes went by, with just the two of them sitting there, holding each other. Kayli shifted against him, moving her head to his shoulder, getting more comfortable. She took a deep breath and let it out.

Ian dropped another kiss on the top of her head, then leaned back just the slightest bit. "Are we still on for our date Friday night?"

Kayli loosened her hold around his waist but didn't move. A long minute went by before she spoke, her voice uncertain. "Did you still want to go?"

"Of course I still wanted to go. Why wouldn't I? God, you have no idea how much I still want to go. How much I want to sleep with you curled up against me all night." Ian didn't think he succeeded in keeping the desperation out of his voice because he heard Kayli's brief but soft laughter against his shirt. But he *was* nearing desperation. He loved the time he spent with her, but he wanted more. He was surprised at how much he wanted the intimacy of her in his arms all night, how much he just wanted to sleep next to her and hold her close and not worry about appearances. Or Jake. Or Lori and the she-devils.

"We could just go to your house, you know. You don't need to actually take me anywhere."

"What?" Her suggestion surprised him so much that he actually pushed her away enough to look down at her. "You're serious! No. No way. As tempting as that may be, no. Friday night is our date night. I told you--I want to wine and dine you. I want to take you out on the town and have fun. So forget about suggesting just going back to my place."

"If you're sure--"

"Yes, I'm sure." He guided her head back to his shoulder and readjusted his arms around her. Then he grinned and dropped a kiss on her forehead. "We can skip the whole date thing on Tuesday night and just go to my place then."

Kayli laughed, as he hoped she would. She needed laughter, and he was happy to be able to give her even a little.

"We should get back to the house." Kayli's whisper was warm against his neck, and he felt himself shaking his head before he knew what he was doing. He shifted, settling her more comfortably against him, and let his head drop against the stall wall.

"Not yet. Let's just stay here for a little longer, okay? I just want to hold you for a little bit more."

He felt Kayli's head nod, felt her body relax more fully against him. Ian smiled and closed his eyes, thinking they would stay here just a few minutes longer, knowing that no matter how long they stayed, it wouldn't be long enough for him.

#

"It's too much, Lori."

"No it's not. You're just not used to wearing it so you think it is."

Kayli blew out a breath and looked back at her reflection in the mirror, trying to be subjective. Lori was right, she wasn't used to wearing much make-up--especially not eye make-up. And how desperate was she that she was actually taking advice from a fourteen-year-old girl?

Obviously pretty desperate.

She glanced at her watch then sighed when all she saw was her empty wrist. She wasn't wearing her watch because it didn't go with the dress or heels or hair or make-up and...it was time for her to take a deep breath before she collapsed into a pile of quivering nerves.

It was just a date with Ian, for crying out loud. It wasn't like they were just meeting for the first time, or that she had to impress him.

But she *wanted* to impress him.

God, she was in such deep trouble.

"Hey Kayli, Ian's here!" Jake's voice echoed up the stairs, making her jump. She took one last look in the mirror, pushed a loose strand of hair behind her ear, then walked out of the room, Lori and the twins behind her. She stopped at the top of the stairs and turned, literally bumping into the girls.

"My purse," she explained at their bewildered looks. Lori laughed and handed her the small black bag. Kayli wasn't sure why she was even taking it with her--it wasn't like it was big enough to carry anything besides her id. And the lipstick and compact Lori made her put in it.

She clutched the bag in her hand and made her way down the stairs, holding onto the railing until she reached the last step. She took another deep breath and smoothed the front of the dress, resisting the urge to pull the hem down. It wasn't terribly short, reaching just above mid-thigh, but between the length of the dress, and the daring neckline, she felt a little self-conscious, a little exposed.

"Ian's in the living room--whoa. Wow." Jake stopped so suddenly that Cole bumped into him from behind. She took a steadying breath, telling herself she would not get emotional at having both of her brothers together. Yes, they were both still sporting bruises and cuts from the other day, and yes, there were still some moments of serious tension. But they were both here, and they were trying.

And right now, they were both staring at her with such weird looks that she almost ran upstairs to change. Then Cole smiled, a broad grin that only briefly lit his eyes. "What happened to our little sister?"

Kayli smiled back, but she couldn't keep the tremble from her lips. "Is it too much?"

Jake shook his head then leaned his shoulder against the wall, watching her. A shadow passed through his eyes but quickly disappeared. "The big brother in me wants to say yes and make you go put on sweatpants and a turtleneck but...no, it's not too much. I'm just not used to seeing you clean up, that's all."

"Gee, thanks."

Jake pushed himself away from the wall and walked over to her, leaning down to give her a quick peck on her cheek. "That's what big brothers are for. Alright girls, say goodnight to Kayli then let's go. Time for the camp out."

"But Dad--"

"No buts. We're going to leave Ian and Kayli alone and head for the great outdoors so we can gorge ourselves on s'mores and ghost stories. So c'mon, let's get moving." He herded all three girls down the hallway to the back porch, but stopped and turned back, waiting for Cole.

"Kayli, you really do look great. Now go have fun, and don't worry. We've got everything covered here tonight and tomorrow." Cole glanced over his shoulder at Jake and the girls then turned back to her. "No worries. About anything, okay?"

Kayli nodded, her throat suddenly tight with emotion. Jake and Cole both winked at her then turned and left before she could say anything. Which was probably better, because she'd end up ruining the make-up Lori had worked so hard helping her with.

So she pressed her hand against her stomach, took a steadying breath and stood a little straighter, then turned and headed for the living room. She had barely walked through the doorway when she stopped, her breath catching in her throat when she caught sight of Ian.

He was standing in the corner, studying the array of photographs hanging on the walls and spread out on her grandmother's old sideboard. The photographs spanned more than eighty years, frozen moments of family history that would mean very little to anyone else. Yet Ian was studying each, a small smile lifting the corner of his mouth.

She studied his strong profile, the sturdiness of his square jaw and chiseled cheekbones, the casual sweep of his hair and the way it curled against the collar of his shirt. His suit jacket must have been tailored to fit him so well, the way it stretched across his broad shoulders and down to his tapered waist and trim hips.

He moved to pick up a framed picture, and must have noticed that she was standing there because he stopped and turned. The smile that had been on his face faltered for a brief second as his gaze trailed over her, the heat in his eyes warming her. His smile broadened, lighting his entire face, and he quickly closed the distance between them. He reached for her hand and gave it a squeeze as he leaned down and kissed her, a lingering yet all-too-short meeting of their lips.

"You are so beautiful." Ian's whisper sent a shiver racing across her skin and she offered him a trembling smile, unable to find her voice. His gaze and his words both told her he was being truthful, but standing next to him, she couldn't help but feel a little underdressed.

Kayli had become so used to seeing him dressed down the last couple of weeks, seeing him in his faded jeans and worn-out t-shirts as he helped with mending fences or hauling bales and bags of feed. She had forgotten that he was used to a different lifestyle, a different living standard. Seeing him dressed as he was now, in a classic cut designer suit with Italian loafers and a gold watch, with his hair casually slicked back, brought the differences between them clearly to her.

And she suddenly felt plain, simple. But before she could say anything, before she could step away, Ian wrapped his arms around her and pulled her closer, then claimed her lips in a searing kiss that emptied her mind of anything except being with him. Her hands gripped the lapels of his jacket and she melted into him. A sigh escaped her when he pulled away and ran his hand along her cheek and through her hair, his desire clear as his gaze searched hers.

"I want this night to be just for you. But I still cannot wait to show you off." Ian lowered his mouth to hers for another lingering kiss then pulled away. "Which isn't going to happen if we don't leave. You ready?"

Kayli nodded, still having trouble finding her voice. If Ian thought anything of that, he didn't say, he just wrapped his hand around hers and led her out of the room and outside. Kayli paused at the top step of the porch, her mouth hanging open in surprise.

"Oh my God, is that what I think it is?"

"What?" Ian flashed her a grin, and she didn't doubt for a second that he knew exactly what she was talking about.

There, in the driveway, was a completely restored, pristine, vintage blue 1966 Shelby Cobra. The late afternoon sun glinted off the chrome, and even from here she could see the immaculate interior. She snapped her mouth closed and tried not to stare too hard, but couldn't help it. The car was beautiful. And suddenly she didn't care that it was more evidence of how different their backgrounds and lifestyles were--she just wanted to get in and drive around in it.

"Wow. Just...wow. You actually drove that up here?"

Ian shrugged, and she could have sworn that the faintest of blushes tinged his cheeks. He suddenly reminded her of a little kid seeking approval, and she leaned up and gave him a quick kiss.

"You like it?"

"Oh yeah, very cool. I'm definitely impressed."

Ian laughed and led her down the steps, then walked over to the sports car and opened the door for her. She lowered herself into the seat, her gaze taking in the restored instrument panel, her hand running over the buttery soft upholstery. Ian laughed again as he lowered himself into the driver's seat and started the engine. A light glinted in his dark eyes as he watched her studying the interior, and he shook his head as he placed the car in gear.

"If I had known that all it would take to impress you was this, I would have driven it the very first time I came here."

"And put Shelly and Sara where? I don't think so." Kayli laughed, then settled back in the seat and let herself relax as Ian maneuvered the little car onto the country road and sped off, racing her away from all her worries and responsibilities, if only for a little while.

ELEVEN

Ian's hand around hers was warm, protective. Possessive even. He flashed the hostess a broad smile then led Kayli deeper into the club. She tried to cover her nervousness by looking around at the wood paneling and expensively framed hunt prints. Leather seating areas were arranged in inviting yet private clusters around the dance floor and along the dark walls. Most of the areas were filled by small groups, people relaxing and talking amongst themselves as Latin music surrounded them. Kayli found herself sneaking glances at the different groups, trying to see if she stuck out at all or if she looked different, like she didn't fit in or belong here.

But everyone seemed to be dressed similarly, and she silently breathed a sigh of relief and hoped that maybe this wouldn't be so bad after all.

She had been giddy when they finally arrived at the exclusive restaurant for dinner. How could she not be, after the crazy but freeing drive down here to the city? Ian had laughed at her obvious joy riding in the Shelby, but she knew he had experienced the same sense of euphoria and power--probably more, since he was the one driving.

The giddiness had mellowed to relaxation during the dinner. It spread through her, warming her. She enjoyed everything, from the food and drink to the easy and comfortable conversation with Ian and, finally, to the smoldering looks that grew between them. By the time they had finished dessert, Kayli was positive that Ian was ready to go back to his place.

But he surprised her by saying they were going to a club. A mostly private cigar club to meet some of his teammates. She tried to hide both her surprise and her resurrected nervousness, but apparently didn't do a very good job of either one because Ian pulled her close and told her not to worry. And then, standing right there at the front of the restaurant, he kissed her so thoroughly and so deeply that many of the patrons were staring at them.

Kayli didn't miss the looks from some of the women, obviously wishing that they could trade places with her. It made her feel a bit self-conscious--and even a bit powerful to be the subject of such envy.

Ian squeezed her hand and she knew he had sensed her nervousness again. It was both exciting and terrifying, how well he knew her moods and even her thoughts without her ever saying a word. She offered him a smile that resulted in him leaning down and giving her another kiss, this one brief yet no less intense. He moved his hand and placed it low on her back, gently guiding her to a cluster of sofas and chairs near the back corner. Several people were already seated there, talking and laughing. The conversation faded as they approached, and Kayli stopped herself from fidgeting as five sets of eyes turned to look up at them.

"About time you showed up. I didn't think you were going to make it." One of the men stood and stepped closer, grabbing Ian's hand in a quick shake even as his gaze studied her.

"Believe me, I was tempted. Everyone, this is Kayli. Kayli, this is everyone."

The man who had stood offered her his hand, a warm smile on his face. His grip was firm but comforting, and she felt instantly at ease. "I'm Alec, nice to finally meet you."

Kayli looked at him in confusion at the greeting, but he had already turned away and was motioning to the small group, introducing them one by one, ending with the woman he had been sitting next to. "And this is my wife, AJ."

The woman reached out to shake her hand and offered her a broad smile that instantly welcomed Kayli. She motioned for her to take a seat next to her, and Kayli did, grateful she was no longer the center of attention.

Ian and Alec continued talking, their words lost in the resumed conversations that floated around Kayli. She looked around her, trying not to stare at the others in the small group but helpless not to notice them.

The other couple sitting across from her seemed oblivious. The man had a foreign name, something French, she thought. Jean-Pierre, that was it. The woman with him was nearly sitting in his lap, fawning over him even as she kept sliding inviting glances toward the lone man in the group. Randy, she thought his name was. There was something dark about the way he sat there, brooding. Part of the group but still distant. He must have sensed her gaze on him because he looked up at her, his hazel eyes disconcerting, probing. He tossed back the drink in his hand in one gulp and abruptly stood, mumbling something about going to the bar.

"Ignore Randy. He's the team's resident bad boy and he's in a foul mood tonight, which doesn't help." AJ leaned over, her voice a low whisper that couldn't be heard by the others. Kayli looked over at her in surprise, but still smiled. AJ smiled back, and nonchalantly motioned to the other couple. "And JP has no idea that his date has the hots for Randy. And for every other player on the team who isn't married."

"Oh." Kayli shifted and tried not to stare at the woman, and tried really hard not to wonder if that included Ian. AJ must have sensed what she was thinking because she slid closer and shook her head.

"I'm sorry, that came out wrong. And it most definitely didn't include Ian. Trust me, I've known him for a couple years and he's not like that. Most of the guys aren't."

Kayli didn't know how to respond, so she just nodded and tried not to look uncomfortable, all the while trying to figure out what to say. Ian saved her from further discomfort when he came over and handed her a glass of wine, then sat next to her. He placed his arm protectively around her shoulders, pulling her in for a quick kiss. He smiled against her lips but didn't pull away.

"Don't pay too much attention to AJ. She'll try to convince you that I'm a saint. Besides, she's a reporter--you can't believe anything she says."

"I heard that!"

Ian and Alec both laughed, and Kayli relaxed once more amid their obvious camaraderie. The conversation continued around her for several more minutes, and she was surprised at how easily Alec and AJ pulled her into it. They asked her about her brothers and the farm and the animals, even about Lori and the upcoming fair. It was obvious that Ian had talked about her to both of them, which surprised her.

"So how long have you and Ian been seeing each other?" AJ asked her when the two men got up to get more drinks. Kayli pulled her gaze away from Ian's retreating form and looked at the other woman.

"Oh. Um, this is really only our first date. Well, second I guess," she amended, thinking of the bull roast.

"Seriously?" AJ sat back and gazed at her thoughtfully, the disbelief clear on her face. "From the way he's talked about you, I would have sworn you've been dating for a while. He must really be serious about you, then."

Kayli shifted uncomfortably, not knowing what to make of AJ's words. She wanted to ask, but she didn't want to sound too eager. Or too naïve. AJ finally laughed and shook her head.

"I am so sorry. My mouth has always gotten me in trouble, and I never know when to shut up. It's just that Ian never brings a date anywhere. Ever. So for him to bring you here...well, let's just say that this is where the guys come when they want to dress up and feel important."

"Important?"

"Yeah. Stupid, isn't it? Testosterone poisoning." AJ raised her glass toward Kayli until the two wine glasses clinked together, then took a drink. "Well, I hope I see you some more. When we can be real people instead of playing at all this dress-up."

Kayli laughed, she couldn't help it. The other woman had summed up her own feelings so adeptly. Yes, she was having fun and felt different, all dressed up. But she wasn't completely comfortable, because this wasn't her. She was gratified that she wasn't the only one who felt that way.

The two women quickly became engrossed in conversation, talking about everything and anything, but especially about Alec and Ian. Kayli was listening so closely to AJ's story about some fight during an awards ceremony, and laughing, that she didn't notice the two men had returned until she felt a hand settle at the junction of her neck and shoulder. She started then looked behind her.

Ian was standing behind her, leaning over the back of the sofa, his mouth inches from her ear. Heat filled his eyes as he gazed at her, and Kayli felt an answering warmth spread through her at the look.

"Dance with me?" It was a demand that came out as a question, and Kayli nodded, helpless to do anything but agree. Her heart gave a little leap then beat faster at the smile that lit his face, and she knew, without any doubt, that she was very much in trouble. It would be too easy to fall for this man, with his boyish charm and easy-going manner, with his ready smile and soul-piercing kisses.

He led her to the dance floor and pulled her into his arms, a sultry Latin beat pulsing around them. His gaze held hers as surely as his embrace, leading her through the moves of a sensual slow dance.

And Kayli realized it was too late, she was already falling for him. She only hoped that he wouldn't completely shatter her heart in the end.

TWELVE

Ian looked over at Kayli, illuminated in the dim light of the garage as the door closed behind them. She looked around, her eyes widened in surprise, then over at him.

"You have a McMansion. And an Escalade."

"A mac what?"

She shook her head, a faint tinge blushing her cheeks as she looked away. He leaned across the tiny interior of the Shelby, his hand reaching out to cup her cheek and turn her face toward his. He lowered his mouth to hers in a soft kiss, refusing to let it get deeper for fear that he'd go after her right here in the front seat of the small sports car.

He had been waiting for this all night--hell, for the last few days, no, make that weeks--and he'd be damned if he screwed it up now. He wanted to make love to her, to take his time and romance and woo her.

But it was so hard to wait when she clung to him that way, her mouth surrendering to his, a soft sigh escaping her. Ian pulled away with a groan and pushed open the driver's door, then ran around and opened her door before she could do more than blink in surprise. He grabbed her hand and helped her out, then led her through the garage to the door of the house.

He restrained himself from hurrying. Barely. All he had to do to forget himself was look at her, so he tried not to.

Which didn't work, either. Not when she looked the way she did. He thought it was funny how self-conscious she had seemed all night.

She really had no idea how many heads had turned her way, how many threatening looks he had tossed at different men throughout the night.

That included two of his teammates. Hell, even Alec hadn't been completely immune, which had earned both of them a humorous look from AJ.

Kayli was beautiful. Wholesome and genuine and real and...beautiful. She had a natural glow that came from within, an inner light that drew Ian to her, made him want to claim and protect and shelter her.

Not that she needed protection. She was independent and strong and straightforward and stubborn, not afraid to speak her mind or do what needed to be done. But that only made him want to protect her more. To claim her, to make her his own.

He couldn't stop the smile on his face at the thought, knowing that Kayli would become so indignant if she knew what he was thinking. Yes, her feathers would be just as ruffled as those of some of the hens she kept at her place if she knew what he was thinking.

"What's so funny?" Kayli asked as he finally unlocked the connecting door and pushed it open. Then he wasn't smiling anymore because he pulled her in after him, kicking the door closed as he wrapped his arms around her and crushed her to him, his mouth descending on hers with the hunger he had been holding back all night.

Kayli clung to him, molding her pliant body against his as he deepened the kiss even more, as he swept his tongue inside her sweet mouth, searching, learning, conquering. Her soft curves pressed against him, sweet torture to the hard-on he had been unsuccessfully fighting the entire night. His hands drifted down her bare arms and around to her back, his fingers tangling in the soft strands of her honey-colored hair. He tilted her head back and ran his mouth down the curve of her neck to the tender spot just above her shoulder. She immediately rewarded him with a soft moan that almost undid the last of his restraint, and he had to push himself away from her, had to before he was completely helpless to go further into the house.

"God Kayli, I want you so much. Right now."

Her eyelids fluttered open, revealing the heated daze of beautiful hazel eyes focused solely on him. The breath left him in a rush and he crushed his mouth to hers again for another deep kiss. Her arms wrapped around his neck, and he broke the kiss long enough to lean down and scoop her up in his arms.

She breathed a small squeal of surprise as her arms tightened around him, then she cradled her head against his chest as he carried her through the house and up the stairs to his room. One of her shoes fell off halfway up, and he reached over and pulled the other one off, tossing it on the floor just outside his room.

Then he pushed the door open, his eyes steady on hers as he lowered her to the floor, her body slowly inching its way down his in sweet torture until she was standing. He leaned down to give her a soft kiss then stood back, watching as the dazed expression in her eyes wore off enough for her to notice her surroundings.

She slowly turned to the side, enough for her to look around while he watched her face. Her eyes widened then briefly filled with moisture that she quickly blinked away. Her mouth opened in a small O that she covered with one hand as she took everything in. Her reaction was worth every bit of planning and every penny to see.

The room was filled with roses, bouquet after bouquet on every surface that wasn't covered with burning candles, even on the floor. Rose petals covered the comforter of his king size bed, laid out in the shape of a heart. A stand with an ice bucket and a chilled bottle of wine glowed in the candlelight next to the bed, and two crystal glasses stood on the nightstand, waiting.

Ian closed the door behind him with a soft click then grabbed the remote from the side table and hit a button. Soft music filled the room, the volume perfect for the romantic setting. He put the remote back and took a step toward her, still watching, waiting for her to say something.

He cleared his throat, suddenly nervous, thinking that maybe he had overdone it because she still didn't say anything. He went to take another step toward her then stopped, suddenly unsure of himself. "Do you like it?"

"Do I--?" Kayli turned toward him, her eyes still wide in surprise. "Ian, it's...oh my God, I've never seen...never even imagined...do I like it? Oh my God, how can you even ask..."

He let out the breath he had been holding on a small laugh, certain now that she did like it, that he really had surprised her. He closed the distance between them and pulled her into his arms, clasping her hand in his and resting it against his chest as he led her in a slow dance. She gazed up at him, her eyes filled with emotion.

"I didn't think guys ever did things like this."

He laughed again and shook his head. "They don't. I don't think. Unless they're crazy and trying to impress someone." He was trying to sound casual, to keep it light between them. Kayli gave him an odd look then a bright smile.

"Then you must definitely be crazy."

And suddenly Ian didn't want to keep it light. He didn't want her to think...whatever she was thinking. He didn't want her to think this was just a casual whim or a fancy seduction. He leaned down and pressed his lips against hers for a brief kiss, then pulled away just enough for her to see his unguarded eyes.

"I am definitely crazy. I'm crazy for you, Kayli. I've never done anything like this before, for anyone. I never wanted to. But for you...anything." It was as close as he could get to putting into words whatever this thing was that he was feeling, which was something he hadn't yet been able to think too much about. Kayli's clear eyes locked onto his, and he wondered what she saw, just as he wondered what it was in her eyes that he was seeing.

And then it didn't matter, because she was leaning into him, lifting herself up until her lips brushed softly against his, once, twice, before her mouth closed over his. Ian stopped moving to the music and just held her as the kiss grew and deepened, as her hands came between them and brushed his jacket to the sides. He shrugged it off and let it drop to the floor as her fingers worked at the buttons of his shirt, undoing them one by one. She tugged on the material, finally untucking the shirt and undoing the last button.

Ian clenched his jaw tight and tilted his head back when she trailed her mouth along his jaw and down his neck. Her fingers brushed against his chest as she spread the sides of his shirt apart then reached up and dragged the material down both of his arms, her lips still grazing his skin, trailing fire, burning him wherever they touched.

Her hands roamed lower, moving slowly to undo his belt then the button of his pants. Her palm grazed down the hard length of his erection then slowly back up before she grabbed the zipper and eased it down. Ian's breath left in a rush and he clenched his jaw even tighter as she eased her hands inside the waistband of his shorts and slowly inched them down past his hips. His erection sprung free and she immediately captured it in her hand, smoothing her palm up and down his hard length, slowly at first, then wrapping her whole hand around him and pumping him with long steady strokes that made him groan.

Her lips trailed kisses further down his chest, to his stomach, to his hip bone where she gently nibbled. Then, shit, she was on her knees in front of him, her mouth closing over him, her sweet hot mouth, taking all of him in, her tongue probing and stroking.

Ian groaned and reached around, fisting his hands in her hair as she sucked him, as her hands stroked and squeezed and explored. Tiny moans escaped her and his hips pumped, urging her on. And shit, it wasn't supposed to be like this, it wasn't supposed to be about him tonight but damn, her mouth was hot and insistent, closing over him again and again, demanding, coaxing, teasing and it felt so damn good...

Ian forced himself to step away from her, gritting his teeth against the loss of her mouth even as he reached for her and pulled her to her feet. His mouth closed over hers, his tongue probing and exploring as he gently backed her toward the bed. He freed his wrists from the shirt cuffs and tossed the thing to the side then reached behind Kayli and found the zipper to her dress. He undid it, not bothering to hide either his haste or his hunger for her as he pushed the dress off her.

Only when the black material pooled around her ankles did he pull away from her. His gaze wandered over her, from the fullness of her breasts held in place by the black lace bra, down to her trim waist and the curve of her hips, to the matching lace thong that covered what he wanted the most. He raised his eyes back to hers and almost gave in to temptation when he saw the heat burning in her gaze. But he reached down deep inside himself, searching for patience, reminding himself that tonight was for her.

He reached out and trailed a finger slowly up each of her arms, from her wrists to her shoulders. He eased the straps of her bra down her arms, then sucked in his breath when she reached behind her and undid the clasp. The material fell away with a whisper. Ian stepped closer, his mouth claiming hers as his hands roamed over her, caressing, touching. He cupped her breasts in his hands, feeling their heavy weight in his palms as he brushed his thumbs across her nipples, feeling the hardened peaks tighten even more at his touch.

Ian broke the kiss to drag his mouth down her neck, along her collar bone then down even further until he pulled one hardened nipple into his mouth, teasing the peak with his tongue. Kayli's hands closed over his shoulders and, with a soft sigh, her head fell back, offering him even more of herself.

Ian wrapped one arm firmly behind her back, supporting her, as his other hand drifted down, skimming her side and stomach, down further to the lacy scrap that covered her. He eased his hand lower, between her hot flesh and the soft lace, pushing the material down over her hips to her thighs. He dragged one finger up, brushing against her, teasing her. Kayli's hips thrust forward and her hands tightened on his shoulders, a small moan escaping her.

Ian dragged his mouth away from her breast, skimming the soft underside before kissing his way down her stomach. He straightened, only to ease Kayli back on the bed, just enough so that her legs were still over the side.

Her eyes fluttered open, her gaze unfocused in heated passion. Ian leaned over and kissed her, then stood up. He quickly kicked off his loafers and pushed his pants and shorts down until he could kick them away as well. He reached over to the night stand, yanking open the drawer and pulling out a condom, not wanting to waste time later.

Then he returned to Kayli, his hands caressing her sides, his mouth teasing her breasts and stomach. He drew one finger down her breastbone, down across her navel, down lower to her wet heat. Her back arched at his touch and her hips thrust upward to meet him. He slid his finger inside, heard her moan as her slickness covered him.

Ian dropped to his knees beside the bed and grabbed her hips, dragging her to edge. Her legs opened wider as his mouth closed over her, his tongue flicking against her clit, tasting her salty wetness as his finger slid in and out of her.

She moaned his name, a soft sigh of sound as his tongue licked and swirled and teased her. Her hips thrust against his mouth as one of her hands tangled in the comforter and the other reached for him, searching. He grabbed it and twined his fingers with hers, the smell of crushed roses filling the air around them. His tongue continued exploring, his fingers deep inside her now, teasing. Her muscles tightened around him, holding him still as her back arched. Silence filled the room, holding everything in suspension for a long second as she tightened even more. The silence shattered as her muscles quivered, convulsing around his fingers as she called his name on a cry. Ian showed her no mercy as he continued to kiss her and stroke her, as she shattered against his touch.

Time finally slowed, along with Kayli's harsh breaths. Ian pulled away from her and stood, sheathed himself with the condom then eased Kayli further back onto the bed. He laid down beside her and gathered her into his arms, his mouth possessing hers in a kiss that stole his own breath away. He skimmed his hand along Kayli's side, from her breast down past her thigh, her flushed skin soft and warm against his palm. Her fingers closed over his hand, not stopping him, just holding.

Ian lifted his mouth from hers, his breath ragged, his heart pounding in his chest. He gazed down at Kayli, at her hair spread around her on the bed, at her parted lips and the rise and fall her chest. Her eyelids fluttered open, her eyes slowly focusing on him in the soft candlelight that bathed them.

Ian captured her gaze and held it, his eyes searching hers. He dragged his hand back up along her side, then clasped his fingers around hers and placed her hand against his chest, against his heart. He swallowed, hard, but said nothing, just continued looking into her eyes.

Kayli's tongue darted out and licked her lips as she eased herself up on her elbow. She dragged her hand from his chest, up along his neck to his face. He turned his head to the side and dropped a kiss on her palm.

"Make love to me, Ian. Please." Her words came out in a ragged whisper, hoarse with emotion. Ian groaned in response and stretched out on top of her, bracing his arms on either side of her. He lowered his face to hers, capturing her mouth with his, claiming her as her legs wrapped high around his waist, claiming her with a single hard thrust deep into her welcoming heat. Her hips raised up to meet him and her breath left her in a rush as he sunk even deeper into her.

He pulled out, slowly, then eased back inside her, torturing himself with the exquisite sensation. Kayli's head fell back and her eyes closed, and he stopped, holding himself steady above her.

"No. Look at me Kayli. Look at me." His own voice was hoarse with emotion. She slowly opened her eyes, slowly focused her gaze on him. He lowered his mouth to hers as he eased himself inside her, then pulled out.

Ian broke the kiss, lifting himself further above her, watching her, his gaze holding hers as he moved in and out of her. Slowly, one long thrust after another, her hot passage gripping him as he pulled out.

Kayli raked her hands along his back, holding him, urging him deeper as she lifted her face to his, as her lips grazed against his mouth. "Ian, please..."

Her ragged plea coupled with the raw emotion and need in her eyes dissolved his restraint. He plunged into her, sinking deeper, over and over, losing himself in her wet heat, losing himself in the depths of her eyes.

Kayli held onto him tighter, her face buried in his neck, her breaths a harsh rasp in her ear. She tightened around him and her head fell back, calling his name as she shattered around him.

Ian stilled for a brief second, watching the beauty of her face, her reaction, her need for him. Then he lost control and plunged into her, again and again, harder, faster. His low groan mixed with hers as she cradled him and led him on a trip to their own personal heaven.

#

Kayli slowly came awake, cocooned in a comforting warmth that radiated from the inside out and urged her back to sleep. Part of her wanted to give into it, to just close her eyes again and drift back to sleep.

But the light that seeped around the edges of the drapes was too bright, and years of routine and responsibility refused to let her escape. She shifted and felt strong arms tighten around her waist.

"Not yet." Ian's sleepy murmur rasped against her ear, followed by a gentle kiss on her neck that caused a shiver of delight to travel across her skin. Ian's hand slid up her side, from her waist to her shoulder to her neck, pushing her hair away so he could kiss her again, just below her ear. Her eyes drifted closed as a sigh escaped her, the touch of his lips against her skin feather-light, seductive.

His erection pressed against her bottom and she wiggled closer, feeling Ian's breath hot against her neck. He rolled her over and stretched himself on top of her, capturing her face between his hands. His dark eyes held hers, searching, making her own breath leave her in a rush at the naked desire so clear in their depths.

Desire, and something else she was afraid to examine, afraid to name. Wishful thinking, she told herself. And she closed her own eyes, very much afraid that he would be able to see what she wasn't yet ready to admit, not even to herself.

"Do you have any idea what you do to me, Kayli?" Her eyes fluttered open when he murmured her name in his husky whisper. Before she could catch her breath, before words she wasn't ready to speak tumbled from her lips, Ian leaned down and closed his mouth over hers in a long kiss that robbed her of all thought.

She wrapped her arms around him, holding her closer, her legs opening for him, already poised at her entrance. He tore his mouth from hers with a groan and pushed himself up, stretching to reach across the bed. He cursed, a guttural sound of frustration as he rolled away toward the night stand to grab a condom, knocking over a bud vase in the process.

Kayli laughed at his continued curses, smiling when he finally tossed her a look of mock surprise even as he sheathed himself with the condom. "Laughter was not exactly the reaction I was going for here."

Kayli bit down on her lower lip, trying to smother her smile as he rolled back toward her. Then all laughter died as he stretched his full length on top of her, his mouth possessing hers as he entered in one swift penetrating move. Kayli arched up to meet him, her breath escaping in a heated rush as he filled her.

"I need you, Kayli." He thrust into her again, hard, his eyes capturing hers, demanding that she meet his gaze. "God, I've never wanted anyone the way I want you. I can't get enough of you."

Kayli arched against him, wrapping her legs high around his waist, urging him deeper. "Ian, I--"

His mouth captured hers, swallowing her words before they tumbled free. She closed her eyes and gave herself up to him, her body surrendering to his demands as he eased himself out then plunged deeper, eased out and plunged deeper. Over and over, again, until he pushed her over the edge. The immediate world shrunk to just the two of them as wave after wave of pleasure poured over her, through her. Ian grabbed her hands and held them over head, his mouth hot against hers. His rhythm quickened, becoming almost urgent, sending more waves crashing through her. He pulled his mouth from hers and threw his head back, calling her name in a low growl through clenched teeth. He pushed into her one last time, a shudder racking his strong body, then collapsed against her, his breathing harsh and ragged.

She wrapped her arms more tightly around him, her body still cradling his as slow tremors moved through her. Kayli turned her head, dropping soft kisses along his jaw, her breathing finally slowing. Ian shifted, just the tiniest bit so he was looking down at her, his dark eyes penetrating her with a serious and thoughtful gaze. Kayli thought about the words that almost fell from her lips, thankful now that he had stopped her, whether inadvertently or on purpose.

"Kayli, I..." She held her breath as he paused, his eyes still searching hers. Long seconds went by before he dropped a quick kiss on her mouth and offered her a small grin. "I think I could get too used to this."

Kayli swallowed, hoping her disappointment didn't show in her eyes as she smiled back at him. "Me, too."

His smile faded and he looked away for a second, his expression serious once more. He turned back to her, his mouth opening to say something, and Kayli waited. But he merely offered her another small smile and shifted to her side, then pulled her tightly against him. "Just lay here with me for a little bit, let me hold you while you sleep."

She swallowed back her disappointment and snuggled closer, finally closing her eyes. She would enjoy this time, the here-and-now, and take everything else one day at a time.

THIRTEEN

Kayli pulled up on the lead and closed the latch of the chute, checking for a snug fit before tying the lead off and grabbing the dryer hose. "Okay Shelly, here you go. Do you remember how to do it?"

The young girl offered her a bright smile and nodded before eagerly taking the hose and aiming it at the just-washed heifer. Kayli watched her for a few minutes, offering a few tips until Shelly had the powerful blast of air aimed correctly. Satisfied she was doing it correctly--or as correctly as a seven-year-old could be expected to do it--Kayli moved to the tack area and grabbed another scotch comb and a leather halter. She stepped into the aisle and looked around, searching for Lori and Sara.

The noise level was loud as always. Cattle bawling, the loud hum of dryers, and over it all, shouted conversation. She took a deep breath, inhaling the scents of hay and cattle and fried dough, and smiled. This was the second day of the three-day county fair, and the most hectic day scheduled.

Yesterday was set-up, and fairly laid back once everything had been set. Tomorrow would be laid back until noon, when exhibits were released and everyone moved all at once to leave. But all three girls were showing today, in several different classes, so the pace was a little more frantic.

But it was a good practice run for the State Fair in a few weeks, a fun-filled crazy ten days that officially signaled the end of summer. And it was a good way to keep busy, to keep her mind off the fact that Jake was leaving in a few days, heading back to California.

Please God, just let him being going back to California.

And Bonnie would be back before then, which meant there would be no reason for Ian and the girls to stay at the house. Kayli didn't want to think that far ahead, though, didn't want to think about how different and quiet the house would be with just her and Lori.

How things might change between Ian and her...

She shook the morose thoughts from her mind and looked around, finally spotting Lori and Sara leading the steer from the wash rack. Kayli moved toward them, watching as they maneuvered the large animal into the second chute, waiting to see if they needed any help. But Lori had everything under control, which left little for Kayli to do except supervise and offer advice wherever she was needed.

"Kayli!"

She turned around at hearing her name, and felt her heart do a triple beat when she saw Ian walking toward her. Maybe 'walking' wasn't quite the right word. He was pushing a wheelbarrow overloaded with hay and feed down the aisle toward them, and she could see he was having trouble maneuvering around the chutes and over the different hoses and cords that filled the aisle. The load was off-balance and Ian could barely see over the top--a certain recipe for disaster. Kayli quickened her steps, but still didn't reach him in time to prevent the wheel barrow from tilting when he tried to push it over it a hose. And instead of just letting the load go, Ian tried to catch it. The weight shifted and everything tumbled off.

And took Ian with it.

Kayli halted, her eyes widening at the sight of Ian sprawled on the concrete floor, partially buried under the bales of hay. He pushed a bale from his lap then stared down at his hand. An expression of what could only be described as abject horror crossed his face. His mouth opened, no doubt to let out a string of expletives at landing in a pile a cow manure, then quickly snapped shut. Ian looked around, his eyes taking in all the kids around them, and he rolled his eyes before catching Kayli watching him.

"Don't even say it!"

Kayli couldn't stop the laughter that burst from her, a steady stream of hilarity that brought tears to her eyes. She doubled over, pressing her hands against her stomach for long minutes until she could finally catch her breath. She wiped her arm across her face and closed the distance between them, reaching down to grab one of the loose bales. Ian took it from her and placed it on the righted wheel barrow, then looked around for something to wipe his hands on.

"Sorry, I couldn't help it." Kayli pulled a rag from her back pocket and handed it to Ian. "Are you okay?"

"Yeah." He wiped his hands clean and bundled the rag, looking around for someplace to put it. He finally shoved it in his back pocket with a shrug the grabbed the handles and started pushing again. "So where do you want all this stuff?"

"Over in the tack area." Kayli pointed over her shoulder then helped Ian maneuver around the different obstacles. "But I'm not sure why you brought all this stuff. We already have enough."

"Ask Jake."

Kayli nodded and looked around, searching for her brother, but didn't see him anywhere. "Is that why you two disappeared earlier?"

"Uh, yeah." Ian set the wheel barrow down then grabbed a bale of hay, lifting it out and walking past Kayli to drop it behind the tack area. She watched him, trying to figure out why he seemed distracted.

"Ian, is everything okay?"

"What?" He faced her, his expression blank and distant. His gaze cleared a little when his eyes finally met hers and he offered her a small smile. "Yeah, everything's good. Don't worry about it."

"Are you sure about that?"

"Yup, I'm sure." He leaned forward and gave her a quick kiss. "C'mon, let's get the rest of this unloaded so I can actually watch the girls when they go do...whatever it is they're doing."

Kayli nodded and helped finish unloading, but she couldn't shake the feeling that something had happened, that something had changed.

She just didn't know what.

Or why.

#

"Uncle Ian, you missed one!"

"This one here!" Sara leaned across the table and dabbed a huge drop of green ink on the micro-thin paper. The color pooled and spread, covering three numbers instead of one. Seconds later, someone called "Bingo!", and the crowd erupted in groans as the winning numbers were verified. Shelly leaned over and pulled the losing sheet of numbers off the pad in front of Ian, smearing green ink over the fresh sheet.

Which was just as well, because Ian's mind wasn't on Bingo, on cattle shows, or even on the people around him. He glanced over at Kayli and offered her a quick smile, but it was obvious she could tell he was still distracted.

And after his earlier conversation with Jake, was it any surprise that he wasn't?

His gaze scanned the crowd as people moved around, taking advantage of the brief intermission. If he hadn't been so distracted, he might have enjoyed the novelty of just being here. If anyone had told him a month ago that he'd be sitting down, playing Bingo, he would have laughed.

Worse still...if he hadn't been so distracted, he'd actually be enjoying himself. He had even won an award himself last night, at the cake auction. Granted, it wasn't a real award, just a ribbon thanking him for being a buyer but he had a feeling he'd be displaying the green and white rosette someplace special.

Ian capped the green ink bottle and pushed back from the table, offering Kayli and the girls a brief smile. "I need to find Jake. Any idea where he is?"

"He's probably back with the cattle. Is everything okay?"

"Yeah, I just wanted to talk to him about something." He leaned down and gave Kayli a quick kiss, then stuck his tongue out at the twins when they giggled. Being silly was better than worrying about the concerned look Kayli was giving him, and there was no doubt in his mind that she knew something was wrong.

Damn Jake for making him promise not to tell.

Ian walked away from the mingling crowds, moving toward the areas where the cattle were set-up. The human noises slowly disappeared, replaced by the quieter sounds of shuffling hooves and low bawls, of contented animals munching on feed or hay. His booted steps created a dull echo around him, blending with the other noises to produce a natural backdrop of sound. And Ian realized he felt...normal. Comfortable. Like he wasn't an outsider, like he fit in.

The feeling was almost as disconcerting as the promise he had made to Jake.

Ian shook off the thoughts and quickened his steps to reach the tack area. Jake was filling water buckets but didn't bother to look up. It didn't matter, because he knew Jake was aware of his presence. He closed the distance between them and leaned against the metal post, just watching until the water buckets were filled. They each grabbed two, then took them over to the cattle to let them drink.

"I thought you were playing Bingo with the girls."

"I was, but I guess I'm too distracted to pay much attention."

Jake leveled him a blank stare then switched an empty water bucket for a full one. "Is that right?"

"Yeah." Ian shifted his hold on the bucket, tightening his grip so he wouldn't drop it as the cow dipped her head in further. "Jake, I'm not sure how comfortable I am with this whole thing."

Jake didn't say anything, just gave Ian another unreadable look. Several minutes went by as the cattle finished drinking. Jake stacked his empty buckets, then took Ian's and did the same. He placed them off to the side, then reached over and unfolded one of the camp chairs propped in the corner. He took a seat, and motioned for Ian to do the same.

"What aren't you comfortable with?"

Ian swallowed a sarcastic bark of laughter and stared down at his folded hands. Jake made it sound like it was no big deal, when the exact opposite was true. In fact, it was such a big deal that Ian didn't even know where his list of 'uncomfortable' started.

No, scratch that. He did.

"How about lying to Kayli, to start with?"

Jake was quiet for a long time, his gaze distant as he stared at something only he could see. He finally shook his head, whether to clear it, or mentally telling himself "no", Ian didn't know. "I'm not saying lie to her. I don't particularly care for that part myself. I just...I don't want her to know. Not until after I leave."

"Jake, this whole thing...I still don't understand. Why do you have to do it this way? And why not just tell her? You can't think for a minute that she'd have a problem with it."

"I think I know Kayli a little better than you do." The statement was almost like a slap in Ian's face, even though he knew it was true. Jake was her brother, of course he knew her better. But it still stung. And Jake must have realized the effect his words had on Ian, because he waved his hand as if to brush the words away. "She's...she has too much faith in Cole, believes too much that he's really changed. I can't put that much trust in him. I won't. If I do and something happens to me...I just can't."

"I thought you two were getting along."

Jake shrugged and leaned back in the chair, folding his hands neatly behind his head. "It's more of a wary truce. Definitely on my part, probably on his part, too. I can't just forget everything that happened like Kayli has. I can't make myself trust him like she does."

"But you'll trust me?"

Jake turned his head and met Ian's questioning gaze head-on. There was such an intensity in his eyes that Ian finally looked away, unable to bear it.

"Yeah. I do."

Jake's answer surprised him as much now as it did yesterday when he first brought the idea up to him. And Ian was just as uncomfortable--just as confused--now as he was then. "What about Lori? Can't you just sign it over to her?"

But Jake was already shaking his head in answer, just like he did yesterday. "It doesn't work that way. Like I told you, I already checked into it. I can't just sign it over to any family member, and if something happens to me, it goes to the next surviving direct family member. That's Cole. And I can't let him have two-thirds control of everything. I just can't."

"But what if he really has changed?"

"I'm not willing to take that chance. There's too much at stake. The only thing I can do is 'sell' my portion, or sign it over to a third party."

"So you won't trust your bother, but you'll trust me? How do you know I won't sell it off to some developer or something?"

"I just know. And if, for some reason, my gut is wrong...I know where to find you." The threat was clear, both in Jake's flat gaze and his steely expression. Ian leaned back in his own chair and closed his eyes, trying to find some way out of this whole mess.

He did not want to be in the middle of this. It wasn't something that he was prepared for, wasn't something he even wanted to be part of. When Jake had approached him yesterday and presented him with the entire convoluted idea, Ian had laughed. Why on earth would Jake sign his portion of the family farm over to him? Ian had thought it was some kind of joke. Even after Jake had explained that if anything happened to him, his portion would automatically go to Cole. Not to

Kayli, not to Lori. To Cole--the brother he had only recently been reacquainted with, the brother he still didn't trust.

When Ian had asked if Jake had talked to a lawyer, to find a legal way around it, Jake had just leveled a flat gaze at him, letting him know that yes, he had already checked.

When Ian suggested that things could be straightened out in the courts, Jake had laughed. Yes, he grudgingly admitted that maybe they could be--even though Jake had already looked into that and was told otherwise. But either way, it would take a lot of money, money that Kayli didn't have to waste to fight a battle she would surely lose.

No matter what Ian said, Jake countered with a valid argument and solid reason. Ian understood his concern, he did. But he sure as hell didn't agree with the idea, and he couldn't come up with a better idea that would satisfy Jake. If he had more time, maybe. But he didn't have more time.

And neither did Jake.

So the only two things he could do was agree to the asinine plan, or say no and walk away.

He felt a nudge on his arm and opened his eyes to see Jake leaning closer to him. He had a thick fold of papers in his hand and was holding them out to Ian.

With a heavy sigh and a feeling of impending doom, Ian reached out and took them, then shoved them in his back pocket.

The time for saying no and walking away was gone.

And Ian knew it had never really been an option to begin with.

FOURTEEN

The screen door closed quietly behind her, and Kayli knew that Jake had held it so it didn't slam shut and disturb the quiet of the night around them. His footsteps moved toward the swing then paused. Several seconds went by before she felt the swing move, felt it shift under his weight as he eased himself onto it. She brushed her cheek against her shoulder, erasing any tell-tale signs of her tears before she opened her eyes and looked over at her brother.

Not that her efforts did any good. She knew from the look on his face that he could tell she had been crying. But he didn't say anything, just offered her one of the bottles in his hand. She took it but didn't sip, just held the cold glass between her hands and watched as Jake gazed out at the dark yard, the silence broken only by the sound of crickets and the squeak of the swing as it drifted forward and back under their weight.

"Lori's finally asleep." His words rang too loud in the night and she watched him grimace as his voice echoed around them. She offered him a small smile then took a sip of her beer.

"She'll be fine."

"Yeah." He took a long swallow then wiped his mouth with the back of his hand. She didn't bother telling him that he didn't sound like he believed it.

The silence stretched around them, speaking volumes without either one of them needing to say anything. Kayli swallowed against the build-up of emotion that grew in her chest, telling herself that she would not, could not, get emotional. Not now, not tonight. This was hard enough on them as it was. So they both sat there, drinking their beers, ignoring the fact that this was Jake's last night home. That he was leaving in the morning.

"So how come Ian hasn't been here?" The sudden question caught her off-guard and she nearly choked mid-swallow. She finished her sip then looked off to the side, afraid Jake would see too much if he could see her face.

"He had to pack the twins up and get them home since Bonnie's back now. That, and he, um, thought we might want some family time before you left." Kayli hoped she sounded more convincing than she felt when Ian had told her that yesterday morning, after he left here with the twins in the recently cleaned and detailed BMW.

But he had left his pick-up behind. Surely that had to mean something.

And even though he had been acting strange since the fair, she had no reason to believe he wasn't telling the truth and no reason to think he was avoiding her. Especially since he had called several times already, just to talk, to see how she was doing.

Yes, he was giving them some family time before Jake left. But she couldn't help but think that this would be easier if he was here instead, even though she knew the distance was probably better for her, anyway.

There were too many new emotions, too many raw emotions, to deal with all at once right now.

"He's a nice guy, I like him."

Kayli smiled and nodded, grateful for the darkness that hid the blush coloring her cheeks. "So do I."

Jake nudged her shoulder playfully. "Yeah? More than like?"

"What? No. I don't know. I haven't known him long enough...no. You're crazy." She quickly took another swallow of beer to stop her rambling, her face heating even more as Jake laughed.

"Hm. I think you might. I'm pretty sure he does."

"Geez Jake, what are you, twelve? Don't be ridiculous." But she was helpless to stop the little thrill that shot through her with his words. Helpless, but not naïve enough to believe them, no matter how much she hoped it was true.

Jake playfully nudged her once more then shrugged, a smile on his face. "I'm just saying." The minutes stretched around them, and Kayli looked over, saw that he was no longer smiling. He was staring down into his beer, a pensive look on his face. He shook his head and brought the bottle to his lips, draining it, then looked over at her.

"Well, if it means anything, I like him. And I trust him. I think, if anything happens...I mean, you can count on him, Kayli. If it's meant to be, I think...just don't be afraid to let someone take care of you for a change, okay? Ian's good for you. You deserve someone like him."

Now it was her turn to look away. She had no idea what to say in response to that, no idea even what to think. So she said nothing, just pushed her toe against the porch and set the swing in motion, letting the soothing sway lull them into a peaceful quiet.

"Ian's taking me to the airport in the morning."

"What?" Kayli turned at his unexpected words, surprised. And a little hurt. "But I thought Lori and I were taking you, to say goodbye on your big send-off."

Jake turned to face her, and she was surprised at the emotion in his eyes as he shook his head. "No more good-byes, Kayli. It's too hard. Tonight, with Lori...I can't put her through that again. Hell, I can't go through it again myself. I'll be gone by the time you two wake up. I'm hoping it'll be a little easier that way, at least for Lori."

Kayli blinked against the sudden burning in her eyes and nodded. Jake had always made his leaving seem easy, always made sure there was enough laughter and carrying on that the other emotions of good-bye and separation faded into the background. She never stopped to think that they were just as hard on him as they were on everyone else.

It wasn't long before Jake stood up with a sigh and moved over to the porch railing, turning so he was facing her. "Kayli, about Cole. I know you think he's changed, but...I don't trust him like you do. I can't."

"Jake, don't--"

"No, I need to say this. If...if something happens, just...think before you trust him too much."

"Jake, I don't want to talk about this right now." And she didn't. She had so hoped that Jake and Cole would make amends, that they could both put the past behind them and start over. They were her brothers, and she loved them both, and she wanted everything to go back to the way it was when they were kids.

And yeah, they had both tried. For her. And she had fooled herself into thinking that everything was fine but it wasn't, not really.

Yes, it was better than it had been...but not like it used to be. She didn't know if it would ever be like it used to be. And she didn't want to be reminded of the rift in her small family, of the tension and mistrust that still existed between Jake and Cole. Not right now, not the night before Jake was leaving, not after being told that he didn't even want to see her in the morning.

But Jake's expression was fierce and serious, and she knew they were going to have the conversation whether she wanted to or not.

"Kayli, please. Just...don't trust him too much." He paused, taking in a deep breath and letting it out slowly. "You need to look out for yourself--for Lori--first. Okay?"

"Jake, don't be ridiculous. Nothing is going to happen. You're only going out to Cali." But even as she said those words, she wasn't sure she believed them. Jake had been quieter than usual at the fair, a little more distant. But surely that was because leaving was getting harder for him, like he just said. There couldn't be another reason. If he was going somewhere else, he would tell her. Jake was going to California, that was all. He would tell her if he wasn't. She had to believe that.

"Promise me, Kayli. Please." Jake's voice was determined, his words pleading. Kayli swallowed and nodded, unable to speak around the lump in her throat. "Thank you."

The quiet night settled around them once more, not quite as peaceful as before. Kayli hated the tension that suddenly hung between them and she struggled to come up with a way to break it.

"Hey." Jake reached out and nudged her foot, and she looked up at him, at the smile on his face and the gleam in his eyes. "Remember when Dad used to take us tadpoling? We used to go up to the pond, betting each other we'd catch dozens?"

"Yeah, and the losers had to do all the chores for the winner for a week."

"Except we never caught any because we were too busy splashing around getting dirty. It drove Dad nuts, because he always used it as an excuse to go fishing so Mom wouldn't yell at him."

"Oh please. Mom knew what he was doing. She was using it as an excuse to get us out of the house so she could have some peace and quiet."

Jake straightened and looked at her with a quizzical expression. "Really? I never knew that."

"Because you men never think. Duh." Kayli laughed, feeling like she was twelve again. Then her laughter faded as the gleam in Jake's eyes brightened. He sat his empty beer bottle on the railing and tossed her a challenging look.

"Bet I can catch more."

"Cannot."

They stared at each other for a long second, silently challenging each other. Kayli jumped from the porch swing just as Jake moved away from the railing. They bumped into each other, pushing and tugging as they both ran down the porch steps and tore around the side of the house, racing to get to the pond first, their laughter ringing in the night air.

#

Kayli's footfalls were quiet as she slipped into the kitchen and poured a cup of coffee. She took a sip and breathed a sigh of gratification as the hot liquid slipped over her tongue and down her throat. She was thankful that she had thought to program the coffeemaker before finally going to bed last night. If it had been left up to Jake, the coffee would taste like old motor oil.

She wrapped her hands around the mug and made her way through the front room and out to the porch. Jake was standing at the top of the steps, leaning against the post with his back to her. His duffel bag sat off to the side, packed and ready to go.

Kayli swallowed hard, telling herself she would *not* get emotional, then opened the screen door and stepped outside, careful to close it quietly behind her.

"I thought I told you to sleep in."

"Don't be an ass. You're my big brother. I'm not going to let you leave without saying good bye."

He turned to face her, his profile in stark relief against the backdrop of the sunrise. Dressed in his uniform, freshly shaven with his hair trimmed, he already looked different. Serious and battle-ready. The tension that thrummed through him was barely contained under the surface, reminding her that he was so much more than just her big brother. He didn't like to talk about what he did or where he'd been. Seeing him like this reminded her once more that he had seen and done things she couldn't even begin to imagine.

And then a grin broke out on his face and he was her big brother again, dressed and ready to go to work. Except his job was on the other side of the country.

Please God, let it only be on the other side of the country.

"Thanks for the coffee."

"I did it for purely selfish reasons. I can't stand the swill you make."

Jake laughed then turned back around as the sound of a motor broke the morning stillness. Kayli felt a smile break out on her face as she saw the car pull up the drive, and her heart melted when the car came to a stop and Ian got out.

"I'll be damned. He brought the Shelby."

Ian walked toward them, a smile on his face as he looked Jake over then turned to her. He climbed the steps and pulled her into his arms, lowering his head and claiming her mouth in a deep kiss that had her leaning against him.

"Okay, enough already. Save it for when there are no witnesses."

Ian pulled away with a laugh, his right arm still draped around her shoulder. "He gets pretty full of himself when he's all dressed up, doesn't he?"

Kayli laughed and she leaned even closer to Ian, thankful for his presence that was keeping everything light and easy. He still had the keys to the car in his hand, and he tossed them up in the air once, catching them deftly in his palm. Then he shrugged and tossed them at Jake, who nearly dropped them in surprise.

"Well, even if you are full of yourself, I guess I can still let you drive."

"No shit. Seriously?" A boyish gleam lit up Jake's face, and Kayli had to bite back a smile even as she blinked back tears. She looked over at Ian then leaned closer to whisper in his ear.

"Thank you."

He shrugged and dropped a kiss on the top of her head, then moved away and grabbed Jake's duffel bag. He tossed it over his shoulder, pausing long enough to give her another quick kiss and to squeeze her shoulder before making his way down the steps.

Jake turned and faced her, all earlier signs of his boyish charm gone. He looked...older, tired. Resigned. She tried to offer him a smile but it wavered on her face, and she threw herself at him, wrapping her arms tight around his waist, as if she could hold him hard enough and long enough to keep him home.

"I love you Jake. Please be careful."

He hugged her back, his hold just as tight, and dropped a kiss on the top of her head. "I love you, too, kiddo. Take care of Lori. And I'll be back home before you know it." He muttered something else but she couldn't make out what it was over the sound of the blood thrumming in her ears. She swallowed against the lump in her throat and abruptly pulled away, afraid that if he didn't leave now, she'd never let him.

Jake turned and walked down the steps, his back straight, not looking back at her until he reached the driver's side door. Then he turned, tossed the keys into the air and caught them, and gave her another grin. She smiled, grateful again for Ian's thoughtfulness.

The two men were getting into the car when the screen door banged open behind Kayli. She turned as Lori ran across the porch and down the stairs, still dressed in her sleep shorts and t-shirt, her hair flying out behind her.

"Dad! Daddy!"

Kayli moved to go after her then stopped, unwilling to take this goodbye away from Lori. She walked to the lower step and gripped the railing, watching as Lori hurled herself at Jake, as he picked her up and held her, his face buried in her hair.

Ian got out of the car and moved away, giving them privacy. She looked over at him, their eyes meeting across the distance the separated them. Her heart lodged in her throat at the emotion she saw in his eyes, at the tears welling in their dark depths. Their gazes held for a long minute, silent communication passing between them as Jake and Lori said their goodbyes.

Then Lori pulled away and turned and ran back to the house, past Kayli as she bounded up the porch steps and inside, her hurried footsteps loud against the stairs. From inside, Kayli heard a door slam, and knew that Lori had closed herself off in her bedroom. She closed her eyes for a brief second, then opened them and looked back toward the car.

Jake was walking around to the passenger side, pausing to say something to Ian. Ian nodded and clasped a hand on her brother's shoulder, then moved to the driver's side. He got in and started the engine, then backed the car up and turned it around.

Kayli watched as it moved down the drive, her hand still raised in a wave long after it disappeared from sight.

FIFTEEN

Ian paused in the hallway, listening for sounds in the house but hearing only silence. It was if the house itself wanted to leave its occupants in peace, to give them time to come to grips with the emotions of this morning.

This morning was not something he wanted to repeat, ever. The strength involved in saying goodbye like that, of never knowing if there'd ever be another hello...

He understood now why Jake wanted to make sure any loose ends were tied up before he left. And why Jake didn't want to tell them he was being deployed, leaving again in a few days. But the secrets Ian now suddenly possessed weighed on him, and he wondered if he was doing the right thing.

He let out a deep breath and continued through the hallway and out to the back screened porch, thinking that maybe Kayli and Lori were up at the big barn, or maybe the pond. He stepped through the porch door and paused, his gaze moving over to the huge willow tree behind the house. Kayli was laying in the oversized hammock, her hands folded behind her head, her face turned toward the expanse of the back yard. The hammock was as still as she was, and Ian thought that maybe she was asleep.

Or maybe she just wanted to be left alone.

He paused at the bottom of the steps, uncertain, wondering if he should have called before coming over. He hadn't thought to ask earlier this morning, and then, later, he had just assumed she would want some company.

Ian was still standing there, wondering if he should turn around and leave, if he was intruding, when Kayli turned her head toward him and gave him a small welcoming smile.

"Hey."

"Hey yourself." Ian walked over to the hammock and smiled down at her. She shifted, sending the hammock swinging as she moved over to the side, and motioned for him to join her. Ian gave the hammock a dubious look, wondering how he was supposed to climb in without sending them both flying onto the ground.

Kayli laughed then lowered her left leg to the ground, holding the hammock still. "Just ease your butt down and swing your legs onto it."

"Yeah, if you say so." But Ian did as she instructed, clutching the side with both hands as everything shifted with his weight. When he was certain the thing wasn't going to flip, he pulled his legs up and settled back, finally stretching out next to Kayli.

She pushed off with her leg, sending the hammock into a gentle swing, then turned and curled against him, draping her arm across his stomach and resting her head on his chest. He brought his arms around her and held her close, running his hand up and down her arm.

"You okay?" Which was a really stupid question to ask, because of course she was going to say yes. But she surprised him by merely shrugging.

"It's been a long day." She lifted her head to look at him, her eyes quiet and tired. "Thank you for this morning."

He leaned forward to kiss her, just a warm brushing of his lips against hers, then eased her head back down. "There's nothing to thank me for."

"You might think so, but I know better. Jake was impressed that you brought the Shelby and offered to let him drive." Kayli shifted, moving even closer against him, her hand drawing lazy circles on his chest. "He likes you. And he trusts you."

"Yeah?" Ian swallowed at the sudden guilt that clogged his throat. He wanted to ask her if she trusted him, but couldn't drag the words out, not holding the secret he held. So he grabbed her hand, twining his fingers through hers and bringing it to his mouth for a kiss.

Kayli turned, stretching so her face was inches from his. Her clear hazel eyes locked on his, searching. His heart hammered at the open emotion reflected in them, and the seconds dragged around them as he waited to see what she was going to say.

"Yeah. I kind of like you, too." She offered him a quick smile then leaned closer and pressed her lips against his. The kiss started softly, almost teasing, before she deepened it, sweeping her tongue against his lips then delving inside.

Ian tightened his arms around her and pulled her further up his body, settling her comfortably between his legs as his mouth fed on hers. He told himself he wasn't disappointed that she hadn't said more, that he really hadn't wanted her to say more, that it was too soon and he didn't need that kind of attachment or entanglement.

And then he didn't care, because every inch of Kayli's body was pressed along his, teasing, hungry. He wrapped his hands in her hair and devoured her mouth with his, tangling his legs with hers, securing her firmly against him. He tilted his hips, pressing his erection against her, and groaned out loud when her own hips thrust even closer.

"Kayli." His voice was so hoarse, so thick with need, that he barely recognized it as his own. What was it about this woman that made him want to forget everything? What was it about her that made him lose control? Because he wanted nothing more than to drive his cock deep inside her, to possess her, to brand her as his.

And then he did forget where he was, because he tried to roll to the side, to urge her under him, so he could possess and brand her...

The hammock tilted and dipped dangerously and Ian jerked back, automatically pushing her away, closer to the middle. She gave a small squeal of surprise as she rolled to her back, as the hammock continued tilting.

Until it went from a tilt to a roll and cleanly dumped Ian onto the ground. Clear laughter came from above him as Ian rolled to his back and sucked in a deep breath. He let it out slowly, thankful at least that he hadn't had the wind knocked out of him and that he wasn't laying there gulping air like a fish out of water.

"Are you okay?"

Ian opened his eyes to see Kayli stretched out on the hammock, resting on her stomach as she hung half off the damn thing and looked down at him. And while the hammock was slightly tilted, it showed absolutely no signs of trying to dump her on the ground.

He grunted and pushed himself to his elbows, then jumped to his feet. Kayli watched him with a smile on her face, her laughter twinkling in her eyes.

"I don't know what's bruised more: my ego, or the mood." Ian brushed the dirt and grass from the back of his pants as Kayli laughed again. But he noticed that she didn't invite him back to the hammock. In fact, she rolled off it, deftly landing on both feet with absolutely no effort.

Which would have bruised his ego even more except that she stopped to give him a warm hug and an all-too-brief kiss. "Are you hungry?"

Ian grabbed her and pulled her closer, dipping his head to claim her mouth in a ravenous kiss that ended too quickly. "Starving."

Kayli's eyes were hooded and glazed with passion, and Ian felt a small sense of satisfaction at the desire that tinged her cheeks a light pink. She pulled back just a little, putting too much distance between them even though their bodies were still touching. "Then um, we should go get something to, you know, eat."

He opened his mouth to reply but Kayli shook her head and stepped out of his arms, a smile on her face. "I meant food. As in real food."

"I wasn't going to say anything!"

"Yes, you were." The laughter was clear in her voice, and Ian couldn't stop himself from smiling--and not only because she was right. He leaned down and gave her a quick kiss, then stepped back.

"Actually, I was going to offer to take you and Lori to dinner anyway. I thought you guys might want to get out of the house for a little bit tonight. So how about it?"

"Lori's not here."

"She's not?"

"Nope." Kayli shook her head and walked past him, heading back into the house. He followed, staying by her side and holding the door open for her.

"Where'd she go? I figured the two of you would want to hang together or something tonight."

Kayli shrugged then turned into the kitchen. She opened the refrigerator and pulled out a pitcher of iced tea, then reached for a glass. She motioned to him, silently asking if he wanted some, then took out a second glass when he nodded.

"She wanted to go to a friend's house tonight for a sleepover. I figured it might help get her mind off things so I said yes." She handed him his glass, then drank from hers, watching him over the rim. He couldn't read the expression in her eyes, which surprised him.

The quiet of the house descended on them as a dozen different thoughts went through Ian's mind. He didn't have a chance to voice any of them, because Kayli finished her tea and spoke again.

"And I'm kind of hoping that having my own sleepover will help get my mind off things, too."

Ian's mouth suddenly went dry, and he gulped down the rest of his tea. He finally looked back at Kayli, at the invitation in her eyes.

And the hesitation as she cast him an uncertain gaze, as if she wasn't sure of herself, wasn't sure if he would accept her invitation.

Ian put the glass on the counter then walked toward her, closing the distance between them. He reached out and cupped his hand around her cheek, stroking her smooth skin with his thumb before lowering his mouth to hers, brushing his lips gently against hers.

"I'm really hoping that means you just invited me to spend the night. All night. In your bed."

"Nah. I thought I'd make you sleep on the sofa again." The corners of her mouth lifted in a teasing smile. "Of course I meant all night. In my bed. If you want to, that--"

Ian silenced her with a quick kiss. "I want. Yeah, I definitely want."

"Good. That's good." Kayli stepped out of his arms and motioned around the kitchen. "So I guess I'll throw something together so we can eat."

"No, you're not going to throw anything together--we're going out. And then we can cruise around on the motorcycle." He watched her eyes light up at the mention of his bike, and he couldn't help but smiling. He reached out and grabbed her hand, then tugged her through the house and out onto the front porch. The Fat Boy was parked in the shade, next to his pick-up truck, the afternoon sun glinting off the polished chrome. "So you decide. Where are we going to go?"

Kayli looked him up and down, from the collar of his athletic polo, down along the worn denim of his jeans, down to the tips of his scuffed work boots. Her gaze travelled slowly back up and when she met his gaze, there was a glint in her eye. And damn, the lazy travel of her gaze along with the look in her eyes had succeeded in getting him worked up again. He wondered if she knew he was standing there with half a hard-on.

From the smile on her face, he guessed she probably did.

"Do you like ribs?"

"Yeah, why?"

"There's a tiny place down in Cockeysville. Great ribs and crab cakes."

"Works for me. Let's go."

He waited for her to go back in and grab her keys and close the door, then led her off the porch and across the yard to the bike. He straddled the machine and kicked it to a start, then motioned for her to get on.

Kayli climbed on behind him, her thighs pressed tight against his legs. She wrapped her arms low on his waist, her entire front pressed against his back.

Ian sucked in his breath when her hands drifted down to his hips as she grazed the back of his neck with her lips. He had no idea where they were going but he hoped that it was a good distance away because he was really enjoying the feel of Kayli behind him on the motorcycle, enjoying the way she clung to him and touched him as he sped out of the drive.

He only hoped that he didn't become so distracted by the feel of her hands that he dumped the bike with both of them on it before they got there.

#

Ian stopped the tractor and brushed his forehead against his shoulder, wiping the bead of sweat away. Not that it mattered, because the heat and bright sun guaranteed he'd be sweating until at least this evening. He reached down for the jug of water near his feet and brought it to his mouth, taking a long drink and not caring that some of it spilled down his shirt. Why he was even wearing the damn thing, he didn't know.

Oh wait, yeah he did. Because he hadn't worn a shirt yesterday while he was helping cut the hay, and his back was now fried. Which is what he deserved for trying to show off his bare chest to Kayli while he was working.

Although he wasn't sure if he was actually helping, or just making a mess of everything.

Kayli had shown him how to use the tractor, and what was involved in cutting the hay. It had looked easy enough. In fact, he figured if Kayli could do it, he shouldn't have any problems at all. He thought it was going to be just like mowing a lawn.

Except a multi-ton, aging, temperamental behemoth of a tractor was a far cry from a riding mower. Even Kayli admitted the aging equipment made the job more tedious than it should be, that a newer tractor would make life much easier. He wanted to ask why she just didn't get a new one, but stopped himself just in time.

He knew why: the damn things were expensive, more than he would have thought. And he knew Kayli didn't want to spend the extra money, to borrow against the property to buy it, not when this one was working.

Ian toyed with the idea of just going out and buying one for them. After all, he had a stake in everything now. Except he didn't, not really, no matter what Jake had made him agree to.

Besides, he knew Kayli would never agree to it. First, he knew Kayli would go through the roof if he did something like that. She would look at it like it was a hand-out and insist on paying him back.

And then he'd have to explain to her about what Jake had done, had made him agree to. He knew she'd find out sooner or later, knew he'd have to tell her because it wasn't right keeping something so important from her. But he was honest enough with himself to admit that he really wasn't looking forward to that conversation.

So he'd have to make do with the old behemoth and worry about everything else later.

Ian capped the jug and placed it back by his feet, then coaxed the tractor into gear, holding his breath, waiting for the engine to engage before he eased it forward. Every single outlandish and insulting thought he had ever had about having it easy living in the country, about this kind of work being easy, came back to taunt him.

Yeah, the last few weeks had really altered his impression of reality. Never again would he think of simple country living as 'simple'.

He couldn't even begin to imagine how Kayli kept this all up on her own. Yeah, she had some summer help--a few local teenage boys that came in for a few hours each day. But still...it was pretty much her and Lori.

And sometimes Cole.

At least now he somewhat understood her love, her passion, for this place. It had been in her family for generations, and while she didn't really talk about it, Ian knew she worried about its upkeep, worried about what would happen if something happened to Jake.

Except Jake wasn't an owner anymore--it was Ian. And again he fought with himself, knowing he'd have to tell Kayli, sooner or later. His gut screamed at him that he had to tell her. If she found out before he told her...he didn't even want to think of the consequences.

Because she would be right. Whatever she thought, she would be right.

And that was probably the absolute worst part of running this aged tractor--it gave him too much time to think. Training camp started next week, the same time as the State Fair, which meant they wouldn't be able to spend as much time together. He just hoped that he'd be able to figure something out, or at least come up with a way to tell Kayli, before then. Either one, Ian didn't really care which.

He had called his accountant, who just happened to be married to his teammate Nikolai, for advice. He didn't know all the details of her past, just that she used to do some kind of work for the government, forensics or something fancy like that. If anyone could figure a way out of or around this mess he had gotten himself into, surely Bobbi could. Isn't that what the big Russian was always saying? His Bobbi could do anything.

Ian hoped like hell that was true.

A shout from his left pulled Ian from the rambling travels of his thoughts, and he stopped the grumbling rust bucket to look over. Kayli was a few feet away, straddling the ATV, waving her arms at him. Ian cut the engine and watched as she climbed off the four-wheeler and made her way over to him, a small smile on her face.

"Am I screwing anything up?" Ian looked over his shoulder behind him, almost afraid that he had done something wrong. Then again, he doubted if Kayli would be smiling like that if he had.

"Nope. In fact, I'm impressed. We'll make a country boy out of you yet!" She climbed up on the seat next to him and pressed her warm mouth against his for a deep kiss. His arms came up automatically and wrapped around her, pulling her closer until she was nearly in his lap. She broke the kiss with a laugh and pulled away.

"Is it lunch time yet?" Ian didn't care that his voice was hoarse--a condition he had come to accept whenever Kayli kissed him like that. Probably because it meant he was ready to be treated to a creative means of making love. Because even though he pretty much stayed here every night, they did not share the same room.

Or the same bed. Not with Lori in the house. Which Ian understood and respected completely, despite Lori's giggles and eye-rolling that let both adults know they weren't fooling her.

"Mmm, not yet, no. I came up to tell you that you have company down at the house."

"What? Who?"

Kayli shrugged then motioned for Ian to move over. "I think some of your teammates. I recognized that guy, Randy. And the guy with the funny French name."

"Jean-Pierre. French-Canadian."

"Yeah, him. And some big scary guy that I could barely understand. I think he's Russian or something."

"Nikolai." Ian bit back his excitement. The fact that Nikolai was here could be good news. Or not. Especially if Randy and JP were with him. But why else would they bother showing up?

"Go on down and see what they want. I'll finish up here." She nudged him off the seat, settling herself comfortably in the spot he had just occupied. Then she turned toward him, her lower lip pulled between her teeth as she studied him. "So I was thinking. I know you have training camp getting ready to start. And we usually have a bonfire right around then anyway. You know, just a little thing before getting ready for the fair and all that. Anyway...do you think you'd want to invite some of your friends? I mean, I should have said something earlier but I didn't think...I mean, if you think they might like it, you can invite them, too. It would be fun."

Ian smiled at her hesitation with the uncertain invitation, and leaned down to give her a quick kiss. "It would be fun. Thank you, I'll ask them. As soon as I figure out what they're doing here." Ian straightened, then tried to climb over her legs so he could get down from the tractor.

Her hands gripped his hips, holding him in place as he straddled her lap. Ian looked down into her upturned face, unable to move, heat searing his entire body at the lazy look in her hooded eyes. She inched her head forward, just the smallest bit, and pressed her mouth against the zipper of his jeans as she cupped his ass in her hands, holding him steady.

His breath left him in a rush and he clenched his jaw at the instant hard-on even as she pulled away and looked back up at him with a mischievous grin. "Good. Because when you're done, I think I might be ready for lunch."

Ian muttered something incoherent under his breath and scrambled down from the tractor, Kayli's laughter following him as he made it to the four-wheeler. He looked back at her with a smile, making her a promise with his eyes of a lunch to remember, then started the ATV and headed down to the house for what he hoped was a productive--but very quick--meeting with his teammates.

SIXTEEN

They were in the front room, milling around and generally looking out of place as they waited for him. Ian glanced at Nikolai, but the big guy was too busy studying all of the old pictures of Kayli's family to notice him.

Randy and JP stopped their grumbling and looked up when he finally walked in, and JP actually laughed.

"Holy shit, Donovan. You look like a refugee farm boy."

Ian looked down at himself: worn dusty jeans, scuffed work boots, sweat-stained t-shirt, grungy baseball cap. Yeah, compared to how JP and Randy were dressed, he did look a little worse-for-wear. But he shrugged off their laughter with his own smile, not caring. "I was working."

He moved his gaze to Nikolai, who was still standing in the corner, his expression thoughtful. Ian tried to gauge what was going through the big Russian's mind, hoping he had good news for him, but Nikolai's face was carefully blank.

"So your new girlfriend has cattle, huh? What kind?" The question came from Randy, and actually surprised Ian.

"Um, a mixed bred market something or other. Why?"

"Cross-bred market steers? Beef cattle? Is she looking to sell any?"

"Yeah, I guess. What do you care?"

Randy shrugged, a nonchalant gesture that was so out of character for the brooding player that Ian just continued to stare. "I might be looking to buy some."

That response caused the other three to gape at him. JP was the first to speak. "Why would you want to buy cows?"

"Not cows. Steers. For the restaurant."

Ian snapped his mouth shut. "What restaurant?"

JP shook his head, a grin on his face. "Randy just spent a fortune investing in a stupid restaurant, thinking it will help his love life. He's not thinking clearly."

The two began their usual bickering and Ian quickly tuned them out, turning once more to Nikolai with a questioning look. Nikolai stepped closer and slowly nodded, and Ian pumped his fist in a victory shake.

"Hey Ian." A voice interrupted before he could ask for details, and he turned around as Lori walked into the room. She stopped, her eyes widening the smallest bit as she looked at all four men.

A teenage boy stood by her side, his arm draped casually around her shoulders. Ian narrowed his eyes and glared at the kid, who abruptly moved his arm with an audible gulp. It was the same boy from the bull roast they had gone to a lifetime ago. Dylan, he thought the kids' name was. Ian made a mental note to find out what was going on with the two of them.

And maybe even have a talk with the kid.

Unlike Dylan, whose expression had gone from one of discomfort to one of excited recognition, Lori was obviously unimpressed with the small gathering of testosterone in front of her. She dismissed them with the aloofness only a fourteen-year-old girl could manage and turned back to Ian. "Where's Aunt Kayli?"

"She took over cutting so I could come back here. What's up?"

"Oh, nothing. I just...we were wondering if we could go for snowballs."

"Sure. Give us another hour and we should be finished--"

"Dylan said he could drive us now, so we don't have to bother you guys."

Ian's gaze shifted back to the boy, whose face was now turning a blotchy red. There was no way in hell Ian was going to let this kid take Lori anywhere. No way. He shook his head.

"No, I don't think so. Just wait a bit and we can all go. Together." He pinned the kid in place with a narrowed look and took perverse pleasure in seeing the boy shuffle his feet in discomfort. Ian turned back to Lori and offered her a smile. "Can you do me favor?"

"What?"

"Randy here might be interested in buying some cattle. Why don't you take him and JP up to your aunt so they can talk business?"

The kid looked less than enthused about the idea, but Lori just shrugged and waited as the two men stood and headed toward the door. JP stopped next to Ian on his way out, giving him a frustrated glance.

"You so owe me for this one."

Ian waited for the four of them to leave, holding his breath until the back door slammed shut. He turned back to Nikolai. "What did Bobbi say?"

"I like this new woman of yours. She is strong. She believes in family."

Ian blew out his breath on a huff of impatience. "You got all that just from looking at some pictures? Great. Glad you approve. Now what did Bobbi say?"

Nikolai placed the picture he had been studying back on the shelf then fixed him with a steady gaze for so long that Ian actually became uncomfortable. Just when he was ready to ask the big Russian what was going on, Nikolai sat down in the stuffed chair, motioning for Ian to have a seat on the sofa. He leaned forward, his usually loud voice quiet in the stillness around them.

"Bobbi will call with you the details. She sent me here first, to see what I can find."

"Find? What are you talking about?"

"She believes you are...what did she say? Crazy."

"Crazy? She said I was crazy?" Ian leaned back on the sofa and looked at his friend in confusion. "Why did she say I was crazy?"

Nikolai laughed, a brief hearty bellow, and made a wild motion with his hands. "Because you did this thing first and questioned later. Because you do not know what you got into. Because you did not think. She says she is tired of fixing problems for men who do not think. So yes, you are crazy."

"I'm not crazy. Yeah, okay, so maybe I should have asked her first but...I'm not crazy. I did it to help out, and I'd do it again if I had to." Ian was surprised at the conviction in his words as they fell from his mouth. And he was even more surprised at how much he meant them. He turned to look back at Nikolai, his mouth set in a grim line. "Now, is Bobbi going to help me fix this, or not?"

Nikolai grinned then sat back in his chair. "Tell me. This woman of yours...you love her." It came out as a statement, not a question, and Ian was instantly defensive.

"What? No. Don't be ridiculous. We haven't known each other that long. I mean, we're just...together. Love? No, of course not." But guilt and uncertainty swept over him even as he denied it, leaving a hollow feeling in the pit of his stomach. He didn't love her. He had strong feelings for her, yes, but love? No. He couldn't.

But Nikolai merely laughed at his protests and shook his head. "So foolish. You should not deny what you feel, and you should not deny telling her. You say you do not love her, yet you are willing to do this thing so she is taken care of."

"That doesn't mean I love her," Ian quickly corrected, and immediately wished he hadn't because Nikolai fixed him with a disbelieving look. Yes, he wanted to help Kayli and her family, was willing to go far to make sure nothing would happen to them. That much he was serious about. But to say he loved Kayli?

No. Love had nothing to do with it.

But Nikolai shook his head again, conveying his disbelief and disappointment in that one small movement. He waved his hand between them, dismissing the argument, then got serious again. "I have seen enough. I will tell my Bobbi, if this is what you want?"

"Of course this is what I want."

"Then Bobbi will call you, and make everything right. But I also believe she is right, and that you are crazy."

#

Soft light flickered from beside the bed, not quite bright enough to chase away the shadows from the corners. Night sounds drifted through the open window with the breeze that fluttered the gauzy curtain. Kayli blinked against the sleep that still held her in its lull, knowing something was different, that something was out of place, but not quite yet sure what it was.

A soft shuffling came from the corner of the room, and Kayli's eyes opened wide as she pushed herself to a sitting position. Her pulse pounded in her ear as her eyes focused on the shadows.

"It's just me." She could barely hear Ian's whisper, even though he was mere feet away. Kayli sat up even straighter and watched as

Ian came closer, lowering himself next to her on the bed. He reached out and brushed the hair away from her face, his hand cupping her cheek as he just sat there and watched her, his eyes intent and serious.

"What are you doing here? I thought you had some things you had to get done."

"I just needed to see you. I didn't mean to scare you."

Kayli shook her head, in part denying he had startled her, in part trying to convey her confusion at his mood. He seemed...too serious, worried almost. She reached up and covered his hand, lacing her fingers through his. If she hadn't been watching his eyes so closely, she would have never seen the shadow that passed over his face. "Ian, did something happen? What's wrong?"

But he merely shook his head, his eyes still intent on hers. He pulled his hand from hers and reached up, once again capturing her face, with both hands this time. He dragged his thumb along her lower lip, and her eyes drifted close at the sensual touch.

"Kayli." He said her name on a soft breath just as his lips brushed against hers, soft, warm, inviting. "Kayli, I need you."

Her eyes fluttered open and the breath left her in a rush at the look smoldering in the depths of his eyes as he searched her face. His need was clear; need, and something even more intense.

He continued to search her face, his gaze intense as his hands caressed her cheeks and tangled in her hair. She held her breath, mesmerized by his touch, by the heat in his eyes. He leaned forward, brushing his lips against hers once more, the touch feather light and seeking. Kayli wrapped one hand around his neck and pulled him closer, holding him in place as she fisted her other hand in the soft cotton of his t-shirt.

Ian deepened the kiss, his passion exploding, surrounding her, consuming her. Her skin ignited wherever he touched: her neck, her arms, her chest. She felt the slight tremble in his hands as he dragged them lower and grabbed the hem of her shirt. He slid the material up, slowly, his palms skimming her flesh and leaving flames in their wake.

He pulled his mouth from hers with a soft groan, his lips hot and moist against her neck and jaw. "Kayli, God...I need you. I need to make love to you. Now."

He pulled her shirt over her head and gently lowered her to the bed, following her down, the weight and heat of his body comforting against hers. The fire raged on, consuming her further, and she fought against it despite the need building inside her.

"The door..." She managed to push the barely audible words past her lips as Ian's hands caressed her, touching, igniting, promising.

"Already locked." Ian abruptly pulled away and stood, his eyes intent on hers as he pulled his shirt off in one quick move. He undid his jeans and pushed them off, his moves slower, his gaze smoldering as he watched her watching him. He sheathed himself with a condom then joined her in the bed, stretching the length of his body next to hers. And still he watched her, his gaze dark, his eyes piercing as he trailed the fingers of one hand from her neck down.

Kayli's back arched and her body tightened, instinctively reacting to his touch. With a harsh breath, Ian rolled over on top of her, capturing her hands with his and stretching them above her head. His eyes held hers as he positioned the hard length of his cock at the entrance to her moist heat.

"I can't wait Kayli. I need you. Now. I need to be inside you. Now." He thrust into her with one fast move, filling her, possessing her. Kayli bit down on her lip to keep from screaming, her eyes closing as her head fell back, intent only on feeling, only on being with Ian.

"Look at me Kayli. Please." The harsh whisper echoed in her ear, demanding. She forced her eyes open, forced them to focus on Ian's face only inches away, even as her body responded to his, meeting his demanding thrusts, demanding in return.

He thrust once more, pushing her to the edge, then stilled, so deep inside her. His eyes held hers, refusing to let her look away, demanding even more than his body. She tightened her hands around his, squeezing, searching for a solid anchor in the sudden maelstrom that threatened to sweep her away.

"Kayli." His lips brushed against hers, the soft touch a direct contrast to the hardness of his body against her, inside her. His eyes blazed in the darkness as he watched her.

She shook her head, not knowing what he wanted, knowing only that he kept her at the edge, that he had the power to hold her back...or send her soaring. Kayli rocked her hips against him, needing to fly, only to have Ian press her more deeply into the mattress. A small shudder went through her, a small promise of what was to come, if only Ian would set her free...

"Kayli." He said her name again, his voice softer yet no less demanding. Ian eased himself out of her, slowly, achingly. His eyes held hers for a long minute then, suddenly, he thrust himself deep inside her in one swift move. "Kayli. I love you."

And she exploded into a million fragments, her body coming apart, her heart taking flight. She thought she told him she loved him, in either a whisper or a scream, she didn't know.

She only knew that she was free, that she was soaring, higher than ever before, with Ian by her side.

SEVENTEEN

Laughter and music drifted through the open windows of the house. Kayli smiled to herself as she pulled more containers of food from the refrigerator and placed them on the kitchen table, where they could be unwrapped and taken outside. She looked at everything spread out on the table and wondered if it would be enough. Yeah, it was a ton of food. Any other time, she might worry about where she was going to put the leftovers.

But today, she was wondering if it was going to be enough. Kayli had no idea that Ian's teammates could eat so much. Her smile broadened and she shook her head, thinking that this year's bonfire was going to be one to remember.

And not just because she had fallen asleep in Ian's arms last night while he whispered words of love in her ear. No, she told herself, that had nothing to do with it. Nothing at all.

"What's the big grin for?"

Kayli jumped at the voice behind her and whirled around, her smile growing as Ian walked up to her. He pulled her into his arms and lowered his head for a kiss that had her melting against him despite its briefness.

"Hmm. No particular reason. I just felt like smiling."

"Is that so?" An identical smile lit his own face as he stared into her eyes. She leaned up on her toes, ready to kiss him again.

"Ewww. Is that all you two do anymore?" Lori bounded into the kitchen and stepped around them, shaking her head as she opened and closed cabinet doors. Kayli bit her lip to keep from laughing at the disappointment that crossed Ian's face when she stepped out of his arms and turned back toward the table. She grabbed a large bowl of potato salad and another of coleslaw then handed them to Ian.

"Can you take these out for me?" She turned back to her niece. "Lori, what are you looking for?"

"The thing you use for barbecue sauce. The brush thingy." She opened and closed several more drawers before Kayli finally took pity on her and walked over to the counter. She leaned around her niece and grabbed the utensil caddy, whipping out the large sauce brush and handing it to her.

"Why do you need another one? I already had one out there."

"Because Ian's friend dropped it."

"Friend?" Ian adjusted his grip on the two bowls and looked at both of them. "Who?"

"The one who bought the steers. Randy. He took over the grilling." Lori grabbed the brush and skipped out of the kitchen, leaving Ian staring after her.

"He did what?"

"I guess he took over the grilling." Kayli grabbed the pan of baked beans and turned, expecting to follow Ian out of the kitchen. Instead, he was standing there with an odd expression on his face, staring at her.

"No. The steers. He did what?"

"He bought them. He looked them over the other day when he was here, and he made me an offer this afternoon."

"Oh." Ian shifted the bowls again, a crease forming between his brows as he watched her. "How many did he buy?"

"All of them. Well, the ones I didn't have buyers for, anyway."

"But...why did he buy them?"

Kayli shrugged. "I don't know. Something about a restaurant. I don't really care, though. I got more than double what I would have gotten if I had taken them to auction, and I don't have to deal with the headache of getting them there or taking them to slaughter. And we worked out a deal for more down the road when they're ready." She moved past Ian, expecting him to follow her, then stopped when she realized he was still standing in the same spot. She turned to look at him, her smile fading at the blank look on his face. "Ian, what's wrong? It was a great deal. Are you upset your friend bought the steers?"

"What? No. Of course not. That's ridiculous. I just thought...never mind, it's not important."

"Are you sure? You look upset about something."

"No, really. I'm just surprised, that's all. I didn't think Randy was serious."

"Well, he was. So thank you for sending him up the other day to talk to me." Kayli took two steps back to Ian and leaned over to give him a quick kiss. "It's getting harder to get buyers these days, especially around here. And buyers who will actually pay decent money...that's a definite bonus. So, thank you."

"Yeah, no problem. Glad to help." Ian leaned down to accept her kiss, a small grin lifting the corners of his mouth even as a shadow passed through his eyes. Kayli thought about asking again what was wrong, but the shadow quickly disappeared and he nudged her forward. "Let's get these outside before I drop them. I'll never hear the end of it then."

The crowd outside eagerly greeted them, diving into the additional food as quickly as they could place it on the tables. Kayli looked around, surprised to realize there were more than thirty people gathered around.

Surprised, and inwardly pleased that the diverse group seemed to be getting along so well. When she first suggested that Ian invite his teammates to the party, she immediately started worrying about how the mixed crowd would work. Visions of two separate groups huddling at opposite sides of the yard, staring at each other, had plagued her since she asked. But her worries ended up being for nothing, because everyone was getting along great, enjoying themselves.

Hockey players and hicks. She smiled at the thought, knowing that Jake would call her every kind of hypocrite for even thinking it. And he was right, because if Ian or any of his friends said the same thing, she would have become righteously indignant.

Kayli looked around, searching for Lori in the crowd of teenagers playing an impromptu volleyball game. Jake had been gone for over two weeks and Kayli knew his absence still weighed heavily on the girl, especially since they hadn't really heard from him. She was thankful that Lori had her friends to help keep her occupied.

Much like she had Ian. She looked around, not surprised to see him standing by the grill with a few of his teammates. He seemed to be involved in a deep conversation but looked up and gave her a smile.

Heat immediately bloomed through her, and she smiled back. She couldn't believe how much she had come to rely on him, on his steady presence. Just having him near during the last couple of weeks had helped deal with the pain of separation once Jake left.

She loved him. She wasn't sure when it had happened, couldn't remember one defining moment that sent her hurtling head-first into such dangerous territory. She only knew she loved him.

And she couldn't believe he actually loved her. Last night still seemed like a dream. And if it was...well, she didn't want to wake up. She could remain in this dream-state for the rest of her life and be happy.

The hours passed quickly. The back yard was cleaned up, food packed away and stored before the bonfire started. She sent Ian ahead in his truck to get the fire going, a task that had some of his friends laughing even as they piled into the bed of his truck and went with him. Some of the crowd followed, while others went home, smiling their sleepy thanks.

Kayli took a few minutes to enjoy the peace and quiet of the sudden solitude as the night grew darker, then headed for the upper field. Their annual bonfire was generally a quiet party, attended by a dozen neighbors just relaxing and enjoying a few precious minutes without responsibilities before the hectic preparations for Fair started. This year, more than two dozen people gathered around the fire, sharing stories or just talking. She searched the crowd, seeing Lori in deep conversation with Dylan. She smiled when she noticed that one of Ian's teammates sat close by, like a silent sentinel, watching the younger man as if he had been appointed her niece's guardian.

Maybe he had been.

Kayli looked around again, searching for Ian, but didn't see him in the fire-lit crowd. Her gaze drifted further up the hill, to the big barn, and noticed the light spilling from the half-open door. A grin on her face, she headed toward the barn, hoping she would find Ian there...and maybe surprise him.

Angry voices drifted through the open door as she approached, and she slowed her pace, her ears straining to hear the words. She recognized Ian's voice immediately, tight with strain and anger.

"I don't give a shit, Michaels. You should have asked me first."

"Seriously, Donovan, you need to chill. What's the big deal? I bought some cattle. So what?"

"Ian, Randy's right. You're making this into something it's not."

Kayli didn't recognize the third voice, so she stepped closer, peering through the space between the sliding doors. The three men were standing off to the side, near the empty stalls. Ian, Randy, and a third hockey player. Alec, the goalie. She had met him the night Ian had taken her downtown, and had seen him earlier in the day today, but she hadn't had a chance to speak with him.

She couldn't imagine why the three of them were up here arguing, but she couldn't miss the waves of tension rolling off Ian, even from this distance. She stepped closer, careful not to make any sounds, feeling guilty for spying even as tendrils of doubt and worry pulled at her.

"I don't want her taken advantage of. How do I even know you paid her what they're worth?"

"What? You think I'm trying to cheat your girlfriend, is that it? You really think I'm that big of an asshole? Christ."

Kayli frowned. The conversation didn't make sense, not when Ian already knew how much Randy had paid--because she had already told him.

Apparently Ian realized the same thing, because he stepped back and ran his hands over his face with a loud sigh and shook his head. "No. I don't. You're right. I just...never mind."

"No, not never mind. You drag me up here and throw all these accusations at me--"

Alec stepped forward and rested a hand on Randy's shoulder. "Randy, let it go."

"No, I'm not going to let it go. What the hell is your problem, Donovan? You're acting like you own this place."

"He does."

The bottom of Kayli's stomach dropped, filling her with a blast of icy dread. She blinked her eyes and stared at the three men, knowing she hadn't heard him right. She reached out and pressed her palm against the door, feeling the rough grain of the weathered wood bite into her flesh as she stared, waiting, telling herself she had heard wrong.

That had to be it. She had heard wrong, and Ian was going to laugh and say it was a mistake.

"He what?" Randy looked back and forth between Alec and Ian, and Kayli knew he saw the same expression on Ian's face that she saw, even from this distance.

Discomfort. Guilt.

"Ian owns part of it. Her brother signed it over to him before he left."

"Alec, enough."

"No, I want to hear this." Randy turned away from Alec and stared at Ian. Kayli's pulse thundered in her ears and she swallowed, needing to hear, to listen. "Your girlfriend's brother signed over his part of their farm. To you. Just like that? What'd she say when you told her?"

Ian muttered something too low for Kayli to hear over the thundering in her ears, but Randy's harsh laugh was clear. "Brilliant. So you're just going to keep sleeping with her and sweet-talking her at the same time. And let me guess, while you're at it, you'll tell her you love her, too, right? That gets them every time. And you call *me* an asshole."

Cold numbness swept through Kayli, filling her, settling so heavily in her chest that the mere act of taking a breath hurt. Their words drifted out to her but she barely heard them. Her vision narrowed and she tightened her grip on the barn door to steady herself. Then she pushed away, stepping out of the shadows and walking into the barn, her gazed focused only on Ian.

Silence greeted her entrance as all three men turned to face her. But she paid attention only to Ian, needing to see his face, needing him to look in her eyes so she could see the truth.

But when he finally met her gaze, all she saw was guilt and regret. The cold numbness claimed the rest of her, icing over her heart as she stared at him, closing out the warm memories of his whispered words of love.

Closing out the pain of his lies.

"Kayli..."

She shook her head and stepped closer as Alec and Randy walked past her, leaving the two of them alone. She kept staring at Ian, waiting, still hoping he would say it was a misunderstanding and that she hadn't heard what she thought she heard.

But the truth was in his eyes. Kayli clenched her fists and stared at him, struggling to get words past her throat. "How?"

Silence greeted her question for so long that she thought maybe she hadn't really spoken. Ian pulled his gaze away from hers and looked down at the dirt floor. "Jake signed over his portion before he left."

"Just like that."

"It's not..." Ian looked up at her, something flashing in his eyes. But he shook his head and looked away again. "Yeah, I guess just like that."

The harsh abruptness of his words shredded her, and she took a deep breath against the pain. Kayli looked up into the rafters above them, then over to the empty stalls and the bales of fresh-cut hay. She took another deep breath. "When?"

"I'm not--"

"When, Ian? When did this happen?"

Silence, then the sound of his heavy sigh. "When we were at the fair."

"That long ago? And you're still hanging around?"

"Kayli, it's not--"

"Don't." She cut him off before he could say anything, before he could tell her that his midnight visit and whispered words had nothing to do with any of it. Before he could lie to her.

Again.

She took a deep breath, then another, fighting for control when all she wanted to do was rail and scream. But the numbness still controlled her, muting the edges of her anger. And her pain.

She looked around the barn again, registering the mixed aromas of cattle, hay and dirt. Comfort smells, for as long as she could remember, in a barn that had been standing since her grandmother was a young girl.

A barn on property that had been in her family for generations. Property that no longer really belonged to her family.

But the pain of that loss still paled in comparison to the pain of knowing that Ian's words of love meant nothing. She took another deep breath and looked at a spot over Ian's shoulder, unable to look directly at him. "So, um, I don't have the money to buy you out, you know that. And I guess you'll want us out of here so--"

"Dammit Kayli, I don't...look at me!" He stepped toward her and reached for her arms, pulling her closer until she had no choice but to look at him. "I don't want the property! I don't want anything to do with any of it! I didn't do this for me. I did it for *you*."

She pulled out of his hold and took a step back, folding her arms across her chest and staring at him in silence. Ian shifted and ran his hands over his face, cursing under his breath.

"I told Jake this was a mistake."

"So you're saying this was all Jake's idea?"

"Yes. He's convinced that something is going to happen to him and he didn't want to worry about you and Lori after he deployed and...shit." Ian closed his eyes and stepped back, the color draining from his face.

"What did you just say?"

"Nothing."

"What did you just say, Ian?" The cold numbness morphed into dread and fear at the look on Ian's face. Kayli swallowed against the irrational panic building inside her. "Jake's been deployed again? When?"

"Kayli--"

"When?"

"A few days after he left here."

Kayli wrapped her arms more tightly around herself. Jake was overseas now, God only knew where, doing only God knew what. But she should have known. Jake talked to Lori once a week, usually over the computer, but neither of them had heard from him in the past ten days.

Which meant nothing. Absolutely nothing.

Kayli took another deep breath, forcing the panicked worry to a far corner of her mind, letting her building anger take its place. Jake had been overseas since he left, and Ian had known about it all along. And Ian now owned a third of her family's heritage. Her anger grew at the realization that was dawning on her.

"The last few weeks have been nothing but lies, haven't they?"

Ian straightened, his eyes focusing on hers. "What? No."

"Yes, they have. You lied about Jake. You lied about the property. You lied about...everything."

Ian shook his head in denial, but the guilt was clear in his eyes. "No, Kayli. Not everything. I wasn't lying when I told you I--"

"Don't." She held out her hand, cutting him off, unable to bear hearing him repeat the words. She took a step back, then another, her hand still held out in front of her as if that would stop him. "Just...don't. I don't need to hear any more of your lies."

"Kayli..."

She shook her head and looked around, searching for an escape. This barn had always been her refuge, her place to come to when she needed to be alone, to think.

Except it wasn't her barn anymore. It was Ian's. Bought and paid for with his money and a few lies.

Lies she had willingly believed.

Kayli cast one last look at him, at the desperation in his eyes, then turned and walked out of the barn. She kept to the shadows as she skirted the laughing crowd gathered around the bonfire, then quickened her pace as she headed back to the house.

EIGHTEEN

Kayli pulled on the halter, coaxing the steer into the chute. She tied the halter off and tightened the latch, securing his head before reaching for the clippers. The steer startled at the sound, and Kayli murmured mindless words to calm him. This one was always a little skittish, and the loud sounds and large crowds at this year's fair didn't help.

So she murmured more mindless words, ignoring the other sounds and smells and sights, even ignoring Lori and the twins in the stall next to her, talking quietly amongst themselves and shooting cautious glances her way.

Something they had been doing since they got here two days ago.

Kayli shook her head and tried to lose herself in the trimming and fitting, tried to get her mind empty of everything, tried to let the last few days just...disappear. Kayli told herself it should have been easy, that worse things had happened.

Her heart thought otherwise.

And it didn't help that Jake said she was overreacting.

She finally had a chance to speak with him yesterday--after sending him one short email the night of the bonfire. *I know you're not in Cali. Call me.*

Jake had been surprised that Ian had told her about the property. He was even more surprised that Kayli was upset about it. He didn't view Ian's lying in quite the same light as she did, not when he considered it worthwhile if it meant protecting her and Lori.

She didn't bother to tell him that Ian had said he loved her. It was obvious that Jake was firmly entrenched on Ian's side. He wouldn't understand how she couldn't trust the words, not when they were uttered on top of all the lies. Jake was so wrapped up in making sure she and Lori were 'protected'.

"Dammit, I don't need protection!" She muttered the words on an angry breath and turned the clippers off. Lori and the twins turned to watch her, their expressions confused. She met Lori's gaze then quickly looked away, setting the clippers off to the side.

She pulled the comb from her back pocket and began brushing the steer out, her mind going back to her conversation with Jake. He told her he did it in case anything happened, that it was to protect her and Lori's interests. In the furthest reaches of her heart, she understood that, knowing that Jake didn't completely trust Cole, knowing how her parents had set up the stupid inheritance to begin with.

She understood that, and in some ways, she couldn't fault him for doing what he did. But for Jake to take such a drastic move and sign his ownership over to Ian on blind faith...how did he know that Ian wasn't going to turn around and sell it? Or decide to build a McMansion right smack in the middle of the place?

I trust him, Kayli. Don't you?

Jake's softly spoken question echoed in her memory. Did she trust Ian? Maybe the bigger question was: could she have allowed herself to fall in love with someone she *didn't* trust?

Kayli straightened from combing the steer and blew the hair out of her eyes, trying to release all her frustration and hurt and confusion in that single breath.

Because the answer was no. No, she wouldn't have fallen in love with someone she couldn't trust. But that didn't excuse the lies, no matter what the reason for them.

"Excuse me. I'm looking for Kayli Evans."

The feminine voice startled Kayli and she whirled in surprise, holding the comb in front of her like some pathetic shield. The woman standing in the aisle offered her an apologetic smile, then took a tentative step closer, her eyes surveying the surroundings before coming to a rest on Kayli. "I'm sorry, I didn't mean to startle you. I'm Bobbi Petrovich."

Kayli lowered the comb and quickly swiped her grime-covered

hand on the rag hanging from the chute as the woman offered her own for a shake. Kayli was surprised at the strong grip of the cool fingers, surprised the woman didn't shy away from the dirt and hair clippings and manure surrounding them. "I'm Kayli. Is there something I can help you with?"

The woman stepped back and looked around again, her sharp eyes assessing. "Ian Donovan is my client. I came about the property. Is there somewhere we can go to talk?"

Kayli's breath froze in her lungs as the world shifted, throwing her off-balance. Was this her worst nightmare come true? It had to be. Why else would she be here?

She heard a surprised murmur and something that sounded suspiciously like a giggle from the stall next to her and she quickly glanced over her shoulder at the girls. All three suddenly seemed preoccupied with the deck of the cards they had been playing with. Kayli frowned at them, then turned back to the woman next to her.

She stared at the woman for a long minute then snapped to her senses, realizing the woman had asked to talk. She looked around her, trying to decide if she should say yes, trying to decide where to go for privacy if she did.

Then she decided she didn't really have time. It had nothing to do with denial, nothing to do with putting off the inevitable. If she didn't talk with the woman, then she wouldn't be able to hear whatever bad news she had come to deliver.

Kayli turned back to the girls, who still looked entirely too preoccupied with playing cards. "Sara, Shelly, where's your mom? It's almost time to show. Lori, could you get the other steer ready?"

"But Aunt Kayli--"

"No buts, Lori. Please?"

"Miss Evans, I understand you're busy but this really is important. I only need a few minutes of your time."

"I really don't have time, I need to be in the ring in a few minutes." Damned if she was going to stand on ceremony and let the woman mess up her schedule. She didn't have the time, or the inclination. Let her deliver whatever bad news she had and be done with it, she wasn't going to make it easier on her.

Kayli released the steer from the chute and ran the comb over him once more, then grabbed her show stick and began the walk to the ring. She looked back once to make sure Lori and the twins were following, wondering why they were so giddy, wondering where Bonnie was.

And wondering why the woman was walking along beside her.

But she had to give the woman credit: she didn't seem upset about Kayli's lack of manners. She merely kept pace with her and scrounged through her oversized bag, ignoring the piles of muck and manure on the floor as she pulled out a thick folder.

"Ian said you'd probably be busy so I won't keep you." She thumbed through the folder, then pulled out a folded set of papers. "I just wanted to make sure you got this."

Kayli stumbled to a stop, her eyes focused on the folded papers, her lungs burning from holding her breath. The woman stepped closer, the papers held out in front of her. She tilted her head to the side, watching, and Kayli realized she was waiting for her to take them.

Kayli switched the show stick to her right hand and reached her hand out for the papers. She wasn't surprised to see the trembling in her fingers, wasn't surprised that her heart beat loud and hard in her chest. Her hand closed around the thick stack and she cleared her throat, refusing to look down at them. "What's this?"

"The deed to the property."

Kayli's head jerked up, her gaze narrowing on the woman. "I'm sorry, excuse me?"

But the woman was already closing up her bag and hoisting the oversize thing over her shoulder. She paused and looked at Kayli, her eyes clear but assessing. "It's the deed to the property. Anything secured by the property has been paid, and your brother also accepted an offer to sell his portion. Ian has now signed it over to you."

"But...I don't understand. Why..." Kayli cleared her throat and finally looked down at the papers. Cole sold off his portion? And everything was paid off? It had to be a misunderstanding. Why would Ian...? She unfolded the sheets and scanned the pages, her vision swimming as she read the clear black print.

The property was deeded to Kayli Marie Evans. Her. Ian had signed everything over. To her. Kayli's eyes scanned the rest of the print. The papers were dated a week after Jake had left.

Before Ian had said he loved her.

She blinked against her blurred vision and looked back up. The woman was still watching her, her expression carefully blank. Kayli cleared her throat again and shook her head. "I don't understand. Why did Ian...I mean..." She didn't know what she meant, still couldn't quite believe what she was seeing with her own eyes. It didn't make sense.

"I'm sure Ian would be able to explain it better, but from what I understand, there was some concern about the safeguarding of the property. I believe Ian gave your brother his word that he would make sure nothing happened."

Kayli folded the pages, smoothing the crease over and over as her mind whirled in disbelief. In the background, she heard the announcer's voice over the speaker, calling all first place steers to the ring. She looked up and met the woman's steady gaze, then looked toward the ring and back at Lori, who was watching her carefully. Kayli cleared her throat and turned back to the woman. "I told him I couldn't afford to pay him."

"For...?"

"For...all of this. I can't afford to pay him back."

The woman sighed and adjusted the bag over her shoulder. Her smooth brow creased and Kayli could see her mind working...but she couldn't begin to imagine what the woman must be thinking. Which made her next words even more surprising.

"This is a gift, Ms. Evans. There's no repayment involved." Kayli opened her mouth to reply, but quickly closed it again at the expression in the other woman's eyes. Silence settled between them, and Kayli struggled to find the right words to break it. But the other woman spoke first, her words gentler than before.

"Perhaps we can speak more later. It looks like you need to go."

"I don't understand."

Bobbi shifted the bag, then motioned toward the ring. Kayli looked over, not really surprised that the other exhibitors were already lining up, not surprised that the woman had misunderstood her. Intentionally? But why?

Kayli shook her head, still reeling from the news as her body went on auto-pilot. She hastily shoved the papers in her back pocket with the comb and blindly led the steer into the ring, only vaguely aware that Lori was still standing with the other steer, that Bonnie was nowhere in sight.

But her mind wasn't really on the show ring, or the cattle, or anything else. She blinked her eyes against the moisture building in them and shook her head again, trying to clear it, trying to make sense of everything that had just happened.

Ian had signed the property back over to her. All of it. According to the woman in front of her, it was a gift. Hers, free and clear. No repayment expected or necessary.

That should have made Kayli happy. Ecstatic even. It meant she had less to worry about, less to keep her up at nights. It meant just a little more security for Lori down the road.

She should have been happy. So why was she suddenly filled with a bitter sense of loss?

Kayli swallowed and tried to push all those thoughts out of her head, tried to focus on setting the steer. Shoulders back, head up, eyes on the judge...

Except the judge wasn't even looking her way. In fact, he wasn't looking at any of the exhibitors. His attention was focused behind them, at the entrance of the show ring where some commotion was erupting.

Kayli refused to look behind her, using the time to try to compose herself. But the grumbling and shouts grew louder, punctuated by several giggles and girlish laughter.

"But Uncle Ian, you don't know what you're doing!"

Kayli stiffened at the voice, ringing so clear across the noise. It couldn't be...

She had to be imagining things. It wasn't possible. Kayli didn't want to turn around but she was helpless to stop herself, as helpless as the rest of the exhibitors who were now turning to see what was going on.

Ian was walking into the ring, leading the other steer. And if she hadn't known it was him, she would have had to do a double-take. In fact, she nearly did. He was dressed like many of the other exhibitors: jeans, boots, and plaid shirt. He held the steer's halter lead in his right hand and a show stick in his left, and walked the steer toward her. His eyes never left hers, even as he stopped beside her and set the steer.

Correctly.

Kayli swallowed and tried to look away but his gaze held hers with such a serious intensity that she couldn't. She was aware of the commotion still going on behind them, not as loud as before--except for the girlish giggling that had followed Ian into the ring.

"Ian." Kayli's voice caught in her throat, making his name come out in a hoarse whisper. "What...what are you doing here?"

His steer tossed his head and Ian pulled on the lead then reset him, using the show stick as if he had done this kind of thing before. He nodded at the judge, who was watching both of them with unshielded curiosity.

"So am I doing this right?"

"Uh, yeah. Yes. But Ian..." Her voice drifted off and she looked around them, noticed that the attention of everyone in the ring--and around it--was on them. "I don't...how..."

"I guess I actually picked up something all those days watching you with the girls." He offered her a small smile, just the briefest lift of the corners of his mouth, but his eyes were serious, the expression in them solemn and intent. "I'm not an idiot, Kayli, but I am an ass. I should have told you the truth. I'm sorry."

"Oh, Ian. I don't know what to say." Kayli blinked against the tears, no longer worried about the crowd watching them, or about the steer or the show or anything else except for the man in front of her.

"Kiss her Uncle Ian!"

"Yeah, kiss her!"

Kayli choked back her laughter at the twins' voices ringing so clear above everyone else, at the sudden urging of others in the crowd who seemed to be caught up in the girls' excitement. She shook her head and looked back at Ian.

"You're right, they are she-devils."

Ian gave her another small smile and shrugged. Then his expression turned serious and he moved closer, just the smallest step.

"I love you Kayli."

"Oh Ian." Kayli dropped her show stick and closed the distance between them, wrapping her free arm around his waist and leaning up to give him a kiss. "I love you, too."

Ian grabbed the lead of her steer and tossed both leads to Lori, who was now standing next to them. He wrapped both arms around Kayli's waist and lifted her off the ground, holding her close to him as his mouth descended on hers with an intense ferocity that held nothing back.

The crowd around them broke out in loud applause and cheers

as they separated. Ian lowered Kayli to the ground but kept his arms close around her, holding her tightly against him. And Kayli figured the smile on his face matched her own, that the love in his eyes was a mirror of hers. She tilted her head up and offered him another kiss, a quicker one this time that was interrupted by someone not-so-subtly clearing their throat.

Kayli looked up to see the judge standing next to them, a broad smile on what was usually a serious face. He shook his head then held out the oversized ribbon for Grand Champion. Kayli laughed and took it from him, then turned and offered it to Ian.

"This one's for you. My Champion."

Ian threw his head back and laughed, then claimed her mouth for another kiss. Kayli eagerly melted into his hold as the crowd cheered them on.

Behind them, three girls giggled and gave each other high fives. One of the twins, it was hard for people to tell which one, looked over at the other two and smirked.

"I told you so."

"No, you didn't. I did!" The other twin said.

The older girl put her arms around the younger two and smiled. "No, girls. We all did!"

About the Author

Lisa grew up with an overactive imagination, strong encouragement from her parents, and an insatiable infatuation with the Peanuts gang. That infatuation—along with an impatience she has yet to outgrow—jump-started her love of writing. After all, why should she be forced to wait a whole week to read the stories of her favorite characters when she could create stories for them whenever she wanted?

That love of writing continued to grow, along with all those voices in her head, even during her assorted careers: first as a firefighter with the Baltimore County Fire Department, then a very brief (and not very successful) stint at bartending in east Baltimore, and finally as the Director of Retail Operations for a busy Civil War non-profit.

Lisa currently lives in Maryland with her husband and two sons, one very spoiled Border Collie, two cats with major attitude, several head of cattle, and entirely too many chickens to count.

Please visit her website www.LisaBKamps.com for exciting information on new releases, to subscribe to her newsletter, and just general craziness.

You may also follow Lisa on Twitter @LBKamps, find her on Facebook at https://www.facebook.com/LisaBKamps or reach her via email at LisaBKamps@gmail.com

Amber "AJ" Johnson is a freelance writer who has her heart set on becoming a full-time sports reporter at her paper. She has one chance to prove herself: capture an interview with the very private goalie of Baltimore's hockey team, Alec Kolchak. But he's the one man who tries her patience, even as he brings to life a quiet passion she doesn't want to admit exists.

Alec has no desire to be interviewed--he never has, never will. But he finds himself a reluctant admirer of AJ's determination to get what she wants...and he certainly never counted on his attraction to her. In a fit of frustration, he accepts AJ's bet: if she can score just one goal on him in a practice shoot-out, he would not only agree to the interview, he would let her have full access to him for a month, 24/7.

It was a bet neither one of them wanted to lose...and a bet neither one could afford to win. But when it came time to take the shot, could either one of them cross the line?

Forensics accountant Bobbi Reeves is pulled back into a world of shadows in order to go undercover as a personal assistant with the Baltimore Banners. Her assignment: get close to defenseman Nikolai Petrovich and uncover the reason he's being extorted. But she doesn't expect the irrational attraction she feels—or the difficulty in helping someone who doesn't want it.

Nikolai Petrovich, a veteran defenseman for the Banners, has no need for a personal assistant—especially not one hired by the team. During the last eight years, he has learned to live simply...and alone. Experience has taught him that letting people close puts them in danger. He doesn't want a personal assistant, and he certainly doesn't need anyone prying into his personal life. But that doesn't stop his physical reaction to the unusual woman assigned to him.

They are drawn together in spite of their differences, and discover a heated passion that neither expected. But when the game is over, will the secrets they keep pull them closer together...or tear them apart?

Jake Evans has been in the Marine Corps for seventeen years, juggling his conflicting duties to country and his teenage daughter. But when he suffers a serious injury and is sent home, he knows he'll be forced to make decisions he doesn't want to. Battered in spirit and afraid of what the future may hold, he takes the long way by driving cross-country.

He never expected to meet Alyce Marshall, a free-spirited woman on a self-declared adventure: she's running away from home.

In spite of her outward free spirit, Alyce has problems of her own she must face, including the ever-present shadow of her father and his influence on her growing up. She senses similarities in Jake, and decides that it's up to her to teach the tough Marine that life isn't just about rules and regulations. What she doesn't plan on is falling in love with him...and being forced to share her secret.

CPSIA information can be obtained
at www.ICGtesting.com
Printed in the USA
LVHW02s0323190318
570313LV00001B/84/P